TITANOBOA

JOURNEY TO THE AMAZON

P.K HAWKINS

SEVERED PRESS

HOBART TASMANIA

TITANOBOA

Copyright © 2017 by Severed Press

WWW.SEVEREDPRESS.COM

ISBN: 978-1-925711-05-9

1

As he once again boarded the *Lucky Lucy*, Dr. Hank Newstead reflected again on the smell permeating all around him. There were lots of rivers throughout the world, lots of pristine places that were resisting the encroachment of man, but the Amazon somehow managed to smell unique among them all. Sure, there was the lush greenery and smell of exotic growing things, the sharp scent of fish and murky water and things growing and living beneath the sometimes calm and sometimes roiling surface. But there were also other things, things that could be found nowhere else in the world. There were the pungent odors of flowers and plants that could only be found here, and a deep, almost incomprehensible odor wafting out of the flood waters flowing among the roots of the trees.

All of it was a far cry from the stale, antiseptic scent of labs and academia he was surrounded by when not in the field. And even though he was uncountable miles away from his mailing address, that ever-present smell made him feel truly at home.

"Newstead, you're doing it again," Morgan said.

Hank blinked several times, bringing himself back to the moment. "Doing what again?"

"Doing that brainy, 'I-smell-a-thing,' hippy-dippy shit you do."

"I do not."

"Yes, you do. Every time you come back to the *Lucky Lucy*, you stop and do that and look like a fool, all while making us late. So are you going to get your ass back to packing up the boat, or what?"

Although anyone else would have interpreted Captain M. Morgan's words as gruff and angry, Hank had worked with him so often in the past that he was able to recognize the fondness hidden underneath his words. Morgan was somewhere in his fifties, and while graying hair and thick gray beard reflected that, no one would have otherwise guessed his age correctly based on his toned, rugged body, the product of a lifetime spent ferrying people just like Hank up and down the Amazon River in search of whatever scientific specimens. Morgan had been the first captain Hank had ever hired for an expedition fifteen years ago, and even though Hank had spent half that trip wanting to throttle the aggravating man in his sleep, there had never been any question about hiring anyone else for future expeditions. Captain Morgan knew the Amazon, and he knew how to get them out of predicaments most people wouldn't have imagined. If you hired Morgan, you got an attitude, but you also an untold amount of skill and experience.

Which was quite the opposite of the other people currently crowding around Hank on the dock. He had five students, interns, and undergraduates with him this time, more than he was used to for an expedition like this, and already he was regretting it. As expeditions went, this was going to be pretty routine, and he'd thought that meant he could use that as a learning opportunity for a few of his students. He'd forgotten, however, what it was like being out in the field for the first time, the uncertainty, the awkwardness, the sea-sickness. Already one of the students was throwing up over the side of the dock, and they hadn't even gotten on the boat yet.

As Katherine caught her breath between heaves, her boyfriend Stu rubbed her back and cooed soothing things to her, all while trying to hide the fact that he desperately wanted to laugh his butt off at her predicament. Katherine was the one Hank had specifically invited, given her crazy-high intellect and exceedingly young age – she was only nineteen, yet already an undergraduate – and when she had asked if Stu could come as well, Hank had initially been doubtful. Then he found out that Stu came from a well-to-do family of professional catamaran racers, and Hank had figured it would be good to have another person on the boat that knew how to hold his own on the water. Katherine, apparently, was not as used to the water as he was. Just the slight movement of the dock upon the river had already made her sick to her stomach.

Rounding out the group were Jasmine, Hank's mousy little teaching assistant, Randy, a young colleague of Hank's from the Folger Institute of Amphibian and Reptilian Studies, and Erin. Erin was one of Hank's students, and if pressed, he would have told everyone that Erin was simply here because she had shown such an intent interest in the trip. In truth, Erin and Hank were in a relationship that straddled the edge of ethical lines between teacher and student. Erin's interest in herpetology was actually minimal. She was here only because Hank needed to work out with her exactly where their relationship was going, and to see if they could find a way to do it without any major ethics violations.

Erin was the one who went directly down the dock and immediately stuck out her hand for the captain to shake. "Hi! Erin Gershwin. Hank has told me a lot about you."

Morgan, obviously taken aback by the tiny blonde's friendliness and forthrightness, did something Hank rarely saw him do with anyone else: he actually reached forward and took her hand, giving it two quick pumps before letting go, as though he thought the human contact would result in some kind of flesh-eating disease if he held on for too long. "A pleasure, I guess," he said. Morgan looked back to Hank. "Everything you sent ahead is already aboard. Get your people on already so we can get the hell out of here."

"Don't you want to be introduced to the rest, first?" Hank asked. He couldn't help but smile. This question had become something of a tradition between the two of them whenever they were starting an expedition, as had the answer that Morgan was about to throw at him.

"Introductions are for people who plan on screwing at the end of the night," Morgan said, not even bothering to look at Hank as he gave the customary response. "And I'm not going to screw over a single one of you."

As the captain went about his business doing the final preparations on his boat, Randy came up to Hank and spoke quietly to him. "Dr. Newstead, this guy looks about as trustworthy as I can throw him. We should find someone else."

Hank scowled. "Not only do we not have the time to look for anyone else, but I've lost count of the number of trips I've made with Captain Morgan. I trust him more than I trust some of my own family." *And certainly more than I trust you*, Hank thought, although he didn't dare say it.

"Captain Morgan?" Randy asked incredulously. "That's seriously his name? Sounds more like…"

Randy apparently hadn't noticed the captain coming up behind him until Morgan cleared his throat. "Sounds more like what?"

"Uh…"

"No, go ahead. Make a joke about my name. I don't mind, but only on one condition. It has to be one I've never heard before. If I have, then I'll break your arm."

4

Randy blinked. "I'm sure you wouldn't really…"

He stopped when he saw that both Hank and Captain Morgan were nodding solemnly.

"Um, I think I'll just skip the joke for now," Randy said.

The captain put a meaty hand on Randy's shoulder, gripping it with enough force that Hank saw Randy wince. "Good man," Morgan said, then wandered off again. Once Randy was dead certain that the captain was again out of hearing range, he spoke again. "I would have never approved of this guy if you had asked me first."

"Since when do I have to ask you first, Randy?" Hank asked. Normally, he was able to keep his cool around this guy, but all the tensions of their flight down to South America, not to mention the funding wars the two of them had been fighting for the last several months against each other, were taking their toll on his calm. "I've been doing these expeditions since you were learning your ABCs with Big Bird."

"Yeah, back when your expeditions to gather rare frogs actually found frogs," Randy said. "Look, I told you I don't want to fight about this."

That was a lie, and they both knew it. Randy got off on their rivalry, just as he enjoyed the fact that he'd managed to get the Folger Institute to reduce Hank's funding. Although Hank couldn't prove it, he even thought Randy's only reason for being here was to gather more fuel for the idea that Dr. Hank Newstead was in need of an early retirement. Not that Hank didn't necessarily agree; these expeditions were getting harder and harder on his body, and he still had a respectable income and profession in teaching. But the idea of being forced out of something that had defined most of his life was something he just couldn't and wouldn't tolerate. If Randall Folger wanted a fight out of him, then that's what he was going to get.

"All I'm saying," Randy said, "is that it's okay for you to let someone else take over some of the planning and duties on this expedition."

"I absolutely agree," Hank said.

"Of course," Randy said, then did a double take. "Wait, you do?"

"I do. That's why I've already handed over most of the planning duties to Jasmine."

"Jasmine? Seriously? But she's just your TA. She doesn't have my…" He pulled up short, but Hank knew full well that the man had been about to say *my money*. Not that it was even his money. His grandfather had founded the Folger Institute, and it was his grandfather's fortune that funded all this. In Randy's mind, that meant he was the one who had done all this and deserved the credit. "She doesn't have any experience in the field."

Neither do you, Hank thought. "She knows what she's doing."

"Look, you're obviously not thinking clearly," Randy said. He patted Hank on the back in a gesture that was probably supposed to look good-natured, yet somehow instead came off as demeaning. "We'll talk about this later, after we're out in the field."

Randy walked away before Hank could say anything. Morgan came up to Hank after the little bastard was gone. He lit a cigarette and offered one to Hank, which Hank declined. Hank always declined, and yet Morgan always offered. It was as much a part of their long-standing routine as the "introduction" line.

"Kid's gunning for your job," Morgan said around a puff of smoke. It was a statement rather than a question.

"It's certainly seemed that way for a while now," Hank said.

"You know as well as I do, a lot of accidents can happen out on the Amazon," Morgan said. He said it nonchalantly, playfully, so much that anyone else might not have realized that Morgan was being dead serious. "It would be a shame if something went down and the little rat bastard never came back."

Hank made sure that Morgan was looking him in the eyes as he replied to ensure that the captain knew he was serious. "Nothing is to happen to him. Nothing at all. I don't work that way, understand?"

"Of course I understand," Morgan said. "And I knew you'd say that. Just as you knew I had to offer."

"And just as you know that I'm appreciative in my own way," Hank said.

"Seriously, though, you've got to be getting close to retiring from this kind of thing, right?"

Hank looked at Erin. "Maybe," Hank said. "Maybe it's time for other things. But I get to make that choice, not people like Randy."

Erin saw him looking at her from her place near the end of the dock. Everyone and everything was on the boat now except her, Hank, and Morgan, and as Hank watched, she boarded. Not, however, before giving him the most beautiful smile and a cute little wave.

"Come on then," Morgan said. He put out his half-way finished cigarette on the bottom of his shoe before putting the rest in the pocket of his shirt. "Time to shove off."

Hank followed him, wondering idly if this would really be his last time boarding the *Lucky Lucy* and going out to explore the Amazon.

2

While it was common knowledge that the Amazon River was one of the longest rivers in the world, Hank found when talking to anyone that hadn't been there that they usually didn't fully comprehend its scale. The river itself cut across almost the entirety of South America, while the river's drainage basin covered forty percent of the entire continent. So while it might seem useful to simply say he was going on an expedition in the Amazon, that was about the same thing as going into the Library of Congress and saying he needed help finding a book that had words in it. Randy didn't seem to understand this, as became apparent soon after they were on their way down the river.

"So when are we going to get to the place where there's frogs?" Randy asked.

Even Stu, having the least experience in this region, gave Randy a look that said he thought the guy was an idiot. Hank would have corrected him, but he held his tongue, waiting for Morgan to do it instead. The captain didn't disappoint.

"If that's all you're looking for, then I could probably shove you right off the boat and you might find a few," Morgan said. "That is, if the piranhas don't eat you first."

Randy turned to Morgan with wide-eyes. "Piranhas? Please tell me you're joking."

Hank showed a little pity on him. "He's mostly joking. We will be traveling through areas that have piranhas, but as far as dangers go, they will be minor. For one thing, while they have been known to attack humans and can be flesh eaters, humans are hardly their preferred food source."

Katherine, who had been standing around near the center of the boat trying to get used to the constant rocking, nodded and chimed in. "Recent studies suggest that most piranha attacks occur during the dry season because of a scarcity of food."

Hank gestured at the sky, which had a few clouds in it in the distance. "And despite what it looks like at the moment, we're in the wet season. Also, the areas with the heavier concentrations of piranhas are further down river. For the moment, we're still in Peru, so we won't have to worry so much. It not even until we get deeper into Brazil that we'll have to even pay attention for that."

While Randy may have been an obnoxious jackass trying to take Hank's place, he at least seemed to realize he'd made a major faux pas in not knowing basic information about what they were doing down here. His next question was worded in a way that he probably thought made him sound less ignorant. "How long before we get to our destination?"

"The site we're investigating this time is about a day and a half down the river," Hank said. "From Caballacocha where we started, we'll be headed east along the border between Columbia and Peru, then pass over into Brazil. There's a large island in the middle of the Amazon River that we haven't checked yet for tree frogs. Hopefully, we'll be able to get some samples, live if possible, but if dead is all we find, then we'll need to properly contain them and bring them back up the river to the Folger Institute's local lab."

"So all this is cool and all," Stu said, "but you kind of sound like you don't think you're going to be very successful in this."

"That's because the biodiversity of frog populations in the Amazon has dropped dramatically in the last twenty years or so."

Randy scoffed. "Please don't tell me you're about to go on about global climate change."

Hank glared at him but shook his head. "This is not the place for politics, but I don't even need to get into that right now. The massive number of deaths of frog species throughout the world has less to do with any change in climate than with a fungus."

"A fungus?" Stu asked. "Really?"

Jasmine was the one that answered. "Specifically, there is a global problem with frogs, tree frogs especially, dying from a disease called Chytridiomycosis, which is caused by the chytrid fungus. It's spread all over the world, even into the deepest portions of the Amazon, and although it's not because of climate, it is because of humans."

"That doesn't sound right at all," Randy said. "If all the frogs of the world were dying, I wouldn't have them in my backyard, would I?"

"You're probably seeing more toads in your local area than you are frogs," Hank said, although what he really wanted to say was *Jesus, you're trying to take my spot in herpetology studies yet don't even know the difference between frogs and toads*? "The fungus originally developed in regions where it clung to toads, but the toads developed a natural immunity. Same with a small number of frogs, but most frogs don't have the ability to defend against it. So as human travel has become more widespread, people have been passing the chytrid fungus to areas of the world where amphibious species never had a reason to develop immunity. The result is a mass die-off, and one of the biggest things the Folger Institute is currently studying."

"Oh," Randy said. The tone of that simple word told Hank that the youngest Folger had no idea what his family's money was actually being used for. "So we're trying to develop a cure?"

Erin finally spoke up, her lilting voice providing a welcome distraction from Randy's incompetence. "At this point, curing is pretty much impossible. The fungus has spread unchecked, and any potential cure wouldn't be spread fast enough to save much of anything. Professor Newstead's work now is more about finding ways to slow the spread of the fungus, while at the same time finding samples of endangered frog species that can be kept alive in captivity. That way they may go extinct in the wild, but there would still be living specimens out there in the world."

"Enough lollygagging," Captain Morgan said to the group gathered on his deck. "Anyone who knows how to help keep a boat afloat and doing what it's supposed to do, get your asses in gear and get to work. Everyone else, stay the hell out of my way, would you?"

Hank, having spent enough time on the *Lucky Lucy* to be considered part of the former group, did his part for the next half hour in various cleaning and maintenance of the boat. As he did, the boat went further down the Amazon River and deeper into wilder areas. At this point, they were still close to various towns and villages along the river, but the more they traveled, the more these signs of human habitation became harder to find. This was the Amazon he had dreamed of exploring when he was a young boy.

"Hey," Erin said to him as she walked up to him. He'd been working on cleaning something, but he must have spaced out and just been staring for the last several minutes.

"Hi," Hank said. As always happened when Erin was around, his heart thumped a little harder and his breath moved a little faster. "So how's your first trip to the Amazon so far?"

"Amazing!" Erin said. "And we haven't really done much of anything yet." She said this with her typical infectious smile, but it vanished soon after. "You told me about this Randy guy, but I guess I thought you were exaggerating. Did you know he tried to hit on me while we were coming in at the airport?"

"Did he? Maybe you should take him up on it. At least he's closer to your age. And he's not your teacher, so there wouldn't be any ethical problems."

"Okay, first off? Ew. The dude's a total douchenozzel. I would never have anything to do with him. Second, why do you always do that?"

"Do what?"

"It's like the first thing you always do whenever I come to hang out with you is tell me all the reasons why we shouldn't."

"Well, what can I say? There *are* a lot of reasons."

"None of which I accept as being legit," she said. "This is all because I told you I might like a relationship with you, isn't it?"

"The professor and the student getting together and acting like they can be a normal couple is such a cliché, Erin. You know as well as I do that it won't work out."

"No, I don't. If it's because you were my professor, then you're not anymore. We're more like colleagues now, whether you want to admit it or not. And don't go saying that I'm not because I don't have a degree yet. That would be insulting."

"No, I won't say that."

"So it's got to be the age thing, right? So you're a lot older than me. Big deal."

"Those kinds of relationships never work, Erin."

"If you really believed that, you would be fighting us harder. And you certainly wouldn't have had me come along on this expedition."

"I invited you on this expedition because, well, I'm not sure if it's going to be my last or not. Even if Randy doesn't succeed in his bids to get me out of the institute, I'm just not strong enough to constantly be in the field anymore."

"And maybe it is," Erin said. "That's up to you. But you still wanted me here for it. We both know that. Your last, my first, whatever."

It was easy for Hank to tell himself all the reasons a relationship between the two of them would be a mistake when he was by himself, but when she was next to him, being her ever-persistent and chipper self, it was hard to convince himself that any of those reasons meant anything at all. In the end, he simply enjoyed everything about her, and she apparently felt the same way about him.

"This is supposed to be the point where I'm supposed to kiss you, isn't it?" Hank said.

Before Erin could respond, Morgan called out to them from the door of his main cabin. "Hey, quit with the lovey-dovey garbage for a second and get your asses over here. I'm picking something unusual up on the sonar."

Hank reluctantly pulled away from his girlfriend (was that really what she was? They hadn't actually decided that out loud yet) and went to join Morgan in the cabin. Stu and Katherine had already joined him, while Randy came in soon after. Jasmine, too lost in her own work to even notice that the captain had called, stayed in her current position at the prow of the *Lucky Lucy*. Once the captain was sure he had their attention, he pointed to something his sonar had picked up in the river.

"Thought you should see this," Morgan said to Hank.

Hank looked at the sonar, but Morgan was the one who was used to reading the thing. "I don't know what that's supposed to be."

"It looks like some kind of mass in the river under the water."

"And a very large one, too," Morgan said. "Except here's the thing. I've gone up and down this river more times than I've heard assholes make jokes about my name and rum, and I've never seen this before. It's completely new."

"Some sort of land mass?" Randy asked.

"No," Morgan said. "It's shifting position. Which means that whatever huge thing is below the water up ahead of us, it's living."

3

Hank continued to stare at the image on the sonar. Morgan was right that they could detect subtle movements from it, but the equipment he had on the *Lucky Lucy* wasn't new or advanced enough to give them more than vague form somewhere below the surface.

"Uh, if it's under the water, can't we just avoid it?" Randy asked.

"Why would we want to?" Hank asked. "I certainly can't think of anything it could possibly be. Whatever it is, it could be quite the discovery."

"Yes, but it's not what we're here for, is it?" Randy asked. "I might not be able to tell you what that is, but I can certainly say it's not a frog."

Katherine took a closer look at the image. "Looks pretty amorphous. No definite shape that we can see from here. Maybe it's not one thing, but many. A school of something, maybe? Perhaps a particularly dense group of river dolphins or arapaima?"

Morgan shook his head. "My equipment may not be the best, but it's not that bad. Even packed together, my sonar would still recognize it as more than one object."

As they watched the sonar, the shape shifted so that, for one moment, Hank thought Katherine might have been right. Parts of the form did seem to break off, yet a closer inspection revealed that he was actually seeing something long and thin that had been coiled tight together. And if he wasn't mistaken, one end of it seemed to be coming in their direction.

"Are you guys seeing this?" Hank asked.

Erin ran out the cabin door and yelled in Jasmine's direction. "Jasmine, you better get in here."

"Just a second. I'm not finished with the…"

Before Hank or any of the others could react, the incredibly huge and long form in the water dashed directly for them. Out the window, he caught the briefest glimpse of something disturbing the water just below the surface, something big enough to cause waves.

"Everyone hang on!" Morgan screamed.

While everyone inside the cabin heard him, Jasmine apparently didn't, nor did her position looking at Erin allow her to see the enormous thing coming through the water for them. The waves hit the *Lucky Lucy* before the mysterious creature did, causing the boat to rock beneath Jasmine's feet. She was seasoned enough on these trips that, if that had been all she needed to contend with, she probably would have been alright. Instead, immediately after the wave, something unseen slammed into the boat on the starboard side. Although Jasmine frantically reached for anything she could grab onto, her fingers missed and she toppled off the bow to the port side.

"Jasmine!" Hank screamed. Erin was closest to her, so she was the first one to reach the spot where Hank's teaching assistant had gone over, with Morgan close behind her and Hank following after. Stu stayed back to keep control of the wheel while Katherine huddled low, her face giving every indication that she was about to vomit again. Randy just stood in place, obviously having no clue what he was supposed to do at this moment.

Hank almost expected to see Jasmine gone when he looked over the side of the boat, but instead, she was floating there, whipping her drenched hair out of her face and sputtering for breath. "Holy crap!" she finally said once she had all the water out of her mouth. "What was that?"

"Someone grab a rope," Morgan said. "We need to pull her back in before whatever that was comes back."

"Just keep treading water," Hank said, then called back to Stu in the cabin when he saw that the *Lucky Lucy* was still going. "Keep the boat steady but bring it to a stop, would you?"

Morgan left them to go take the wheel back from Stu while Katherine, despite her wobbly disposition, came up to the side with a rope. They threw it out to Jasmine before she was out of range, and she grabbed on.

"Okay, now pull," Hank said to Erin and Katherine. They both helped him start to reel her in, but until the boat came to a full stop, they were fighting against the water.

"Hank!" Morgan called from the cabin. "Whatever that thing was, it's coming back from the aft side!"

Hank looked back out behind the boat to see that the water was again bubbling with something humongous underneath it. Even as he tried to keep all his concentration on pulling Jasmine in, the biologist in him tried to piece together all the little clues he'd seen already in an effort to identify what the creature might be.

An anaconda? he wondered. No, that couldn't be it. Anacondas might have been the longest currently living snakes in the world, but the biggest ever supposedly on record was roughly eighteen feet long, and even then that measurement was believed by many to be an exaggeration. This thing, whatever it was, was much larger, both in length and girth.

And yet, given what he had briefly seen on the sonar, evidence did suggest that this might be some kind of snake. Except, there wasn't any snake currently living that was bigger than an anaconda. So either this had to be something completely different, or else they were seeing some species that had never before been recorded.

The herpetologist in him almost rejoiced at this thought of seeing a new snake for the first time, before he remembered that his teaching assistant was still in the water with it, and it was coming right for them.

They managed to pull Jasmine right up to the side of the boat. Hank looked back to see the water parting, revealing the great arrow-shaped head of a snake. While the coloring was unfamiliar to him, the size and other subtle aspects of its shape gave him an idea of what it might be. But that was impossible. It couldn't be what he was thinking. Those kinds of snakes had been extinct for...

Well, there was no time to dwell on it. Both he and Erin reached down for Jasmine. She let go of the rope so that she could grab one of their arms in each hand, and with some effort, the two of them yanked her up out of the water. The three of them collapsed on the deck in a single soggy heap, but there wasn't any time to regain their breath. Hank pushed the other two off of him and looked back into the water just in time to see the snake dive deep into the water, leaving only a flick of its tail for them to see before it disappeared altogether.

"Is... is it gone?" Erin asked.

"Sonar shows that it's still coming for us," Morgan called from the cabin. "It's going deeper but... wait. It's coming back up from right below us! Brace yourselves!"

The *Lucky Lucy* lurched as Morgan tried to get it moving at full steam again, but it couldn't get going again in time. Rather than coming from directly underneath the boat, the giant snake rocketed out of the water just to the side, arching up and over the deck at an angle. Hank and Erin managed to duck, but Jasmine was still too dazed from her impromptu swim to prepare herself in time. Hank looked up just in time to see the monstrous snake, probably well over fifty feet long and fully capable of fitting a full-grown human in its mouth, clip Jasmine in the head with the its lower jaw. The thing let out a hiss that echoed out over the waters, and Hank thought it almost sounded frustrated, like it was annoyed at itself for not hitting one of the humans directly. The brief impact was enough to cause damage, however, as the snake's momentous weight knocked Jasmine unconscious and sent her sprawling across the deck. The rest of the snake followed it over the boat, but while the head went clean over the other side and back into the water, the thousands of pounds of giant snake caused its back end to hit the boat before it could follow the rest back into the river. Boxes and pieces of railing and everything beneath it shattered.

And Jasmine got caught right underneath it.

The tail almost pulled her back off the side as it slid off with the rest into the Amazon, but Hank scrambled forward just in time to grab her by the leg. He pulled her back away from the edge of the boat, then carefully went to peek over the side.

"Newstead, you idiot, get away from the edge!" Hank looked back to see Morgan running at him, a machete brandished at his side like he fully expected there to be another attack by the creature at any moment. When Hank looked back into the murky river, however, there was nothing. There was no sign that anything had been there at all, and even the water was calming down. Although the snake still had to be there somewhere, it was giving no indication that it was coming for them again. If it wasn't for the evidence the sonar had recorded, right along with the obvious destruction on the deck of the boat and the slack-jawed expressions of his fellow adventurers on the *Lucky Lucy*, Hank might have thought the entire thing was some kind of hallucination or fever dream from some obscure tropical virus.

"Oh God, Hank?" Erin said from behind him. "Please tell me someone on this boat is a medic." Hank ran back to her side, where she was now kneeling next to Jasmine. While both the captain and Hank had plenty of first-aid training, Hank could tell immediately that there was nothing he could do to save the young woman. Although her eyes were open, there were barely any signs of life there. The colossal bulk of the snake had crushed her thoroughly. All four of her limbs stuck out at unnatural angles, and she was bleeding from multiple compound fractures poking through her skin. The most telling detail of all, however, was the disturbing concave shape of her chest. Her breasts were pushed in, showing just how utterly crushed her ribcage had been, and the blood spewing from her mouth as she took shallow breaths indicated that her broken ribs had probably punctured her lungs in several places.

"Please," Erin said, her words barely recognizable through her torrent of weeping. "You can't just leave her like this."

He could, unfortunately, and even Morgan saw immediately when he joined them that there was nothing any of them could do. Instead, he simply hugged Erin tight against him with one arm, burying her face in his chest so she wouldn't have to look, and held Jasmine's shoulder in his other hand as she took her last breaths.

Bubbles of blood formed at the sides of Jasmine's mouth for the last time, and then she was gone.

4

As far as the lairs of evil villains went, Camp Anthropocene left much to be desired. Dr. Annalisa Sanderton had always kind of had the idea that, if she was to become some mustache-twirling villain (not that she could ever grow a mustache, of course), she would set up shop in some kind of volcanic caldera or create a base at the bottom of the sea. But, in reality, things didn't work out like that. She didn't have the unlimited funds for any grandiose gesture. Instead, Camp Anthropocene was a literal camp, a conglomeration of tents and pre-built shacks and sheds that she'd been able to assemble on the fly in order to do her work. Although it all lacked grandeur, it was all enough to serve her nefarious needs.

Not that Sanderton thought of herself as a "nefarious super villain," or at least not really. Whenever she used those words in her mind, they were firmly in quotation marks, a cheeky way to refer to herself based on how she guessed other misinformed people might think of her if they knew what she was doing. There had been a few that knew, except they were dead now. Not on purpose, of course. Their deaths had been purely accidental. After all, she wasn't *really* a villain. If she considered herself anything, she thought of herself as the hero.

Sanderton wandered around the messy confines of her camp, her mind wandering as she waited for her next set of experiments to finish running. Camp Anthropocene consisted of three tents – one for sleeping, one for supplies, and one that was actually empty, since she'd just had the extra and got bored one day, putting it up for no good reason – and five small buildings. Each of the buildings was the sort of pre-made sheds one could get at a Lowes or Home Depot, although two of the buildings were actually made of several of the sheds put together. These bigger ones were where she kept the live specimens that she hadn't yet released into the wild, while the smaller one was where she actually created the specimens to start with. Each building was hooked up to several portable generators, each one going full steam to provide the proper environment and electricity she needed to keep everything running smooth.

At the center of the camp was a fire pit. When she'd first come here, she'd done everything she could to keep the fire going at all times, since that was simply how she thought these things were supposed to be done. Now, like anything else that wasn't related directly to her experiments, she had neglected it, and it spent most of its time as a trash pit rather than a source of heat. Right now, the pit was heaped high with Twinkie wrappers, as that was the latest crate she had opened and been subsisting off of for the last several days. Once those were gone, she would have to go on to whatever junk food was in the next crate.

See, this is another reason no one could call me the evil mega villain, Sanderton thought. *Villains dine on filet mignon while they watch their minions do all the work. I gorge on things so full of preservatives that they'll probably give me cancer.* She wasn't too overly concerned with her health. In her mind, she was already a dead woman walking. The whole human race was. So there was no point in eating healthy. Better to enjoy the bizarre, pre-packaged creations of humanity while they were still around to be consumed.

Okay, so, given the current state of her camp, she could see how others might think she was on the verge of losing it. Plenty of others already thought that. That was why she was using funding and equipment that she had borrowed (without permission, in most cases, but she still wouldn't allow herself to think of it as stealing) with the help of some major university or think tank. She'd been kicked off the faculty of two colleges and been laughed out of meetings with half a dozen potential donors. They didn't understand what she was doing, although they kept saying they understood perfectly, and that their decisions were more about the unethical nature of what she wanted to do. As far as Dr. Sanderton saw it, though, anyone that thought was she was doing was unethical didn't understand in the slightest. To her, *not* doing what she was doing would be unethical.

Something pinged from inside one of the sheds, telling her that what she'd been working on was finished. She walked around the pile of garbage in the center of camp, carefully avoiding the sonic fence she had set up around the perimeter to keep out the most dangerous of possible predators (or sometimes to keep them in, depending on what phase of her process she was currently on). Once inside the shed, she immediately took a seat on her weather-beaten stool and checked her equipment. In the center of her rather cramped and crowded workspace, there was an incubator with a single large egg inside. She could already tell just from looking at it that this particular experiment had failed, but she refused to get downhearted until after she'd looked at all the readings. Perhaps there was still something here she could learn in an effort to recreate her earlier, completely successful test subject.

Sanderton went over all her monitoring equipment, checking temperature, chemicals present inside the eggs, DNA and RNA stability, and a large number of other things that a layman couldn't begin to understand. The egg she was using this time around was that of an *Eunectes murinus*, more commonly known as the green anaconda, the largest snake that was still supposed to be alive in the world. Using an anaconda egg had worked the first time, but that was the problem now that she was trying to go beyond her earlier success. Even as the supposedly largest snake in the world, the green anaconda was still significantly smaller than the *Titanoboa cerrejonensis* she was currently trying to grow. The previous success might have just been a fluke. While a snake egg should still theoretically be the best vector to grow her new (or rather not so new) species, she might have to start experimenting with other things, such as ostrich eggs.

Not that she could get her hands on an ostrich egg all the way out here, now that she thought about it.

The more she looked at the readings, however, the more she realized that the egg itself wasn't the problem. It was all in her DNA sample. The sample she had used to create her first *Titanoboa* had been unusually intact, far more than she would have ever thought possible from a fossil fragment. That sample was gone now, completely used up to make her first *Titanoboa*.

Of course, that was why she was doing this whole thing in the field in the middle of the Amazon Basin. This was where the sample had been found, so if she was going to continue, she needed to find more. Camp Anthropocene was in the right area, according to everything she had found so far, but the exact location was still a mystery.

Dr. Sanderton pondered all this as she removed the failed egg from the incubator and started the setup for the next one. Truly, *Titanoboas* shouldn't have been the only species she should be concentrating on at the moment, and her other sheds and workspaces were full of other samples, both genetic and in stasis, as well as alive and thriving. She'd even released several of them already, although she'd known she shouldn't. They should all be released at once to create the best impact. But she'd had the itch to see what some of her creations could do, and even though deep down she knew there was a problem with what she was doing, she couldn't get herself to listen to that part.

All at once, Sanderton walked away from what she had been doing and instead went to visit the shed where she kept the live specimens. Upon opening the door, she was greeted by chirps, whistles, hisses, and hundreds of other sounds. She walked among the cages and aquariums full of fish, insects, frogs, reptiles, and mammals, all of which were supposed to be extinct. To the rest of the world at large, every single creature in this shed was gone forever. Some of them were believed to have gone extinct very recently, while others had disappeared soon after humans started walking the Earth. In most instances, the creatures she had genetically re-engineered and brought back from extinction were gone because of human influence. She even had a dodo in one cage, although she didn't think it would live long. Sanderton couldn't get the damned thing to eat. Apparently, some creatures didn't want to continue existing.

She came to the empty cage at the back of the shed. Until recently, that was where she had kept the lone *Titanoboa* she'd brought back to existence. *Titanoboas*, the largest snakes ever known to have lived, were unique among her menagerie in that humans had not had anything to do with their disappearance from the planet. More likely, natural differences in climate and problems feeding them had led to their demise. Nevertheless, Sanderton had known from the beginning that she wanted the giant snake species to be among the creatures in her little zoo here. She had plans for them, plans that pushed her in the minds of others from being merely eccentric and unethical to straight-up villainous.

Some villain she was, though. The one *Titanoboa* she'd

managed to bring back so far had gotten too big for its measly cage and escaped. It was out there somewhere, hopefully wreaking exactly the havoc she had birthed it for, but without it, she couldn't make more. All she had instead was a large empty cage.

Sanderton put her forehead in her hands as though fighting off a headache. There was certainly pain there, but it was entirely of the mental variety, not of the physical. The part of her that could still be logical told her that something was wrong with her, that she wasn't thinking clearly, that nothing she was doing actually made any sense. That part was weak now, though, grown soft through the strange onslaught in her brain.

You were infected with something, remember? she tried to say to herself. *None of this is you. You're twisting your own research into something it's not.* That voice didn't stay for long, however. And as it faded away, she remembered that she was supposed to have all the information she needed to get another sample, something that would allow her to not just create another *Titanoboa*, but many.

And once she did, she could unleash them. An apex predator, capable of killing and devouring massive numbers of humans, unleashed on the population.

Humans wouldn't be the top of the food chain anymore. Then there would just be her, and she could reintroduce as many species as possible. She'd be a hero.

None of that makes sense, Annalisa. You have to stop this. Don't you remember? The prion that was released in your lab? You're not thinking...

She shook her head, clearing away her intrusive thoughts. It all made sense. It would all work. She just had to get back to work and find the genetic sample, the entire reason she was here.

She wandered back to the incubator. She still had plenty of work to do.

5

Hank carefully pulled a tarp over the crushed and broken corpse that was all that remained of his teaching assistant. He'd been on enough expeditions into the Amazon that he'd seen plenty of people hurt, including himself on several occasions, but he'd never seen anything quite as gruesome as this. And in most of those other times, when someone had been injured, it hadn't been someone he'd known as well as Jasmine. Usually, it was just someone he'd hired as help. Instead, here he was covering up the body of someone he had worked with, someone he had considered a friend. His brain simply couldn't respond to this.

Erin, thankfully, stood by his side and held his shoulder as he gave his respects. As much as Hank would have liked to take Jasmine below decks, they didn't have time at the moment. Instead, they all had to do figure out what the hell had just happened, and what they were going to do about it.

"Stu, give me some kind of damage report," Morgan said.

"Uh, things are damaged?" Stu said. "I'm still trying to wrap my mind around this."

"God damn it," the captain said. "Fine. I'll go around and see if that thing did any irreversible damage. Stu, you keep the wheel steady, and keep it going fast. Whatever that was, we need to get away from it as fast as possible."

"Shouldn't we be turning back?" Randy asked. "I mean, one of our people died. You can't seriously expect us to keep going down the river in search of fricking frogs, do you?"

"You better watch your tongue, you little bastard," Hank said. Everyone around him seemed surprised by his tone, Hank included. "My friend just died. Don't you dare act like any of us aren't taking this seriously."

"And to answer your question, do you really think turning back is the best idea?" Morgan asked. "That creature, whatever it was, disappeared from the sonar by going back behind us. That means that it is between us and any help we might have been able to get that way. The smartest thing to do now is simply to put as much distance between it and us as possible." Randy opened his mouth, but Morgan raised a finger to stop him. "And before you try to disagree with me, just save your breath. I'm the captain here, remember. What I say goes. Your job is simply to shut the hell up."

Erin got Hank to look her in the face. "You're the senior herpetologist here. Could you tell any of us what that thing even was?"

"You mean other than a snake?" Hank asked.

"Hey," Randy said. "If I can't be snarky, then neither can you."

Hank let out a deep sigh. "Sorry. I wish I could, but that's beyond anything that I've ever seen."

"What about an anaconda?" Katherine asked him. "You know, like from those movies?"

"Those moves are complete hogwash," Hank said. "Anacondas don't get that big, and they certainly don't get as big as the snake we just saw."

"It couldn't be some variation you've never seen before?"

Erin asked.

"If something that size had been living in the Amazon River on any of my previous trips, I would have seen it," Hank said. "This thing is new, and it shouldn't be here. It's almost like it's a... hmmm."

"What?" Katherine asked.

"The size and general shape do resemble something that once existed in the area now known as Columbia, but that can't be it. Those have been extinct for nearly sixty million years."

"Wait, sixty million years?" Randy asked. "Are you saying we've just run into some kind of dinosaur?"

"No, that was definitely a snake. But it resembled something called a *Titanoboa*, a monster snake from the Paleocene epoch."

"That's nuts," Randy said. "You can't honestly be telling us that some kind of dino snake has successfully been hiding out from humans for millions of years only to show itself now."

"No, I agree. That kind of thing is impossible," Hank said. "I'm just saying that's what it looks like."

"Okay, so humor us then for a minute," Katherine said. "If this creature were in fact a *Titanoboa*, what would that mean for us?"

Hank blew out a breath and ran a hand through his hair. His specialty was modern snakes and amphibians, not prehistoric, but he'd done enough work on paleoherpetology to know a few basics. "Well, to start with, there hasn't been a lot of fossils found to work with, so most of what we think we know about the *Titanoboa* is conjecture. There's some argument about whether it was an apex predator or simply a piscivore."

"Uh, I have no idea what that means," Randy said.

Even Katherine seemed to be getting annoyed now that one of their supposed experts didn't know what he was talking about. "Either it ate everything, or it just ate fish."

"It's a little more complex than that, but that's the basic gist of it," Hank said.

Morgan came back to join them just in time to add something to the conversation. "Given the way it came at us, either it's the first one, or else it thinks the *Lucky Lucy* is a really big fish."

"So is there anything it could possibly be other than a *Titanoboa*?" Erin asked.

"The next largest snake in history is believed to be the *Gigantophis*," Hank said. "But that still would have been at least forty million years ago, and it was believed to measure at only around thirty feet."

"And our new special friend today was definitely longer than thirty feet," Morgan said.

"So what else do we know about this *Titanoboa*?" Randy asked.

"That's it," Hank said. "Even if paleontology were my expertise, there still haven't been a lot of fossils for the *Titanoboa* found anywhere. Although, now that I think of it, I do seem to recall some recent rumors about *Titanoboa* fossils found on an island in the Amazon River."

"And would that island be anywhere near here?" Morgan asked.

"Not too far from where we had originally intended to land for this expedition, now that I think of it," Hank said.

"So is that it?" Randy asked. "We're just spontaneously changing what we're looking for?"

"We're not looking for anything anymore," the captain said. "A member of the crew is dead. I didn't know her from Adam, but I still show some damned respect for the people on my boat. The expedition is over as soon as we can find a safe place to dock."

"And is that going to be anytime soon?" Katherine asked.

"Unless anyone here wants to take a rowboat and go back through the section of river where we met the enormous God-damned snake, then no," Morgan said. "We keep going. We stay safe. And we protect each other. Hank, you've been in a few hairy situations with me in the past. You can do this. And I'm sure the rest of you can too." Morgan looked pointedly at Randy as he said this, like he wasn't at all sure that he was telling the truth about the young man, but Randy seemed oblivious to the scrutiny. He looked like he was too busy feeling miserable for himself that he was in this situation.

"If we were to power straight ahead rather than turning and trying to go back," Erin asked, "how long would it take before we reached any kind of settlement or camp that might be able to help us?"

"Moving at maximum speed? Maybe a week," Morgan said.

"That's ridiculous," Randy said. "Just turn the boat around. That thing can't attack us again, right? As a representative of the Folger Institute – who is paying for this expedition, if I really need to remind you – I order you to do that."

"Kid, you may have the same last name as the people signing my paychecks, but this is my boat, and as long as I'm alive, what I say goes," Morgan said. "Keeping going will be longer, but less dangerous, so that's what we're doing. And if you try to pull your imaginary rank on me again, I will personally dangle you over the side and use you as bait to lure that thing out again."

"No, you wouldn't," Randy said.

Hank cleared his throat. "Ahem. Actually, he would. I've seen him do it." He hadn't, really, but the way Randy suddenly paled was worth the lie.

"So here's what we're all going to do. I'm going to keep us going and alive," Morgan said. "That Stu kid is going to help me. Erin and Katherine, you two go around and try to fix and clean up any damage left by that snake. Professor, you go over that sonar data and anything else we recorded. See what else you can learn."

"What about me?" Randy asked.

"You are going to hide in some deep, dark corner of the boat where I don't have to look at your miserable little face." Then Morgan walked off, and everyone went about their work.

6

"Are you sure there isn't any town or village along here that we could go to?" Randy asked. Although Hank had wondered the same thing multiple times, Randy was the only one who kept asking it over and over, like a child wondering if they were there yet. Despite the captain's order that he hide and make himself as unobtrusive as possible, he was still wandering around the *Lucky Lucy* aimlessly, doing little to help the workings of the boat and generally making a nuisance of himself.

"We passed the last place even slightly resembling a port about half an hour before that thing attacked us," Morgan said.

"If we really just have to keep going straight on," Hank asked, "do we even have enough supplies to make it to the next safe harbor?"

"Before, I would have said yes," Morgan said. "But that snake smashed several of our reserve gas tanks. We have plenty of food, but after a day, we'll be floating dead in the water."

"And there's absolutely no place along the way where we can find supplies?" Katherine asked.

"I wouldn't say that," Morgan said. "There are supply caches here and there in case of emergencies. I and some of the other riverboat captains had them set up for this kind of occurrence. The problem is finding one that hasn't already been used up or pilfered."

"So I assume that's where we're headed first?" Erin asked.

"You assume correctly," the captain said. He said it with a small smile on his face that Hank rarely saw with him. Apparently, Erin had endeared herself to him. It was easy to see why. Once she finished her chores on the boat, she came into the cabin to join Hank as he poured over the sonar data they had recorded on the snake. As loathe as he was to refer to it definitively as a *Titanoboa*, that was the only known creature that fit the description of what they had seen, and the sonar data supported the idea.

"Morgan's sonar isn't the most high tech," Hank said to her as she sat next to him and cuddled close. "But it's enough to show that the *Titanoboa* was about fifty-five feet long. That large mass we saw when it first appeared was what it looks like when it's coiled up. I've never seen anything that size before. It shouldn't even exist."

"Have I told you lately that you're very sexy when you talk herpetology to me?" Erin asked playfully.

Hank fidgeted in his seat. Although he normally liked it when she was in this mood, there was no way to ignore their age difference when she was sitting there practically jazzed by their discovery while he was worn out and tired. It was about time the two of them had a conversation, and while he would have much rather had it anywhere else, it should probably be had sooner rather than later. "Erin, do you think maybe we should break up?"

"If I've told you once, I've told you a hundred times. You can't break up with me, because you've always been too squirrelly to officially declare us as being together."

"Seriously, Erin. Our age difference is kind of ridiculous."

"So? What does that matter? I love you." Before he could

respond, she put a finger to his lips to silence him. "And I know exactly what you're about to do. You're going to go into that whole angsty mode because I just dared to use the L word. You do this whole routine, what, like twice a week? And yet somehow I'm still by your side."

"You make it sound like we've been together forever," Hank said. "It's been six months, depending on how you define when we started."

"Why do we have to define it? I love you, you at least like me, although I suspect one of these days very soon you'll get off your ass and realize you more than just 'like' me. We have fun. Maybe it will last, maybe it won't. But now that I'm not your student anymore, I don't have any qualms about any of this. So why does it still get to you?"

"I guess I'm just worried about what people will think."

"I don't worry, so why should you?"

Hank wished he could answer that question. Erin made it quite obvious that she had no problem with their May-December romance, and Hank's relationship with his colleagues was practically non-existent, so it wasn't like it mattered to him what they thought. He just couldn't shake the idea, though, that what they were doing was somehow wrong. It had been drilled in his head most of his life that this sort of relationship was unacceptable, so no amount of logic that said otherwise could ease the distress it caused in his head.

Hank continued to analyze the sonar data, but he didn't make much headway as the day passed. They had gone quite some distance by the time the light started to fail, and everyone on the boat, even the captain himself, was exhausted. Randy, Stu, and Erin retired to the tiny bunks provided for them just below deck, while Katherine continued keeping a watch on the water just in case the *Titanoboa* was sighted again. Captain Morgan and Hank stayed in the cabin, where the captain pulled out a bottle of rum and a couple of glasses for the two of them.

"Do me a favor and skip the traditional jokes about me drinking while piloting the boat," Morgan said.

"Not really in the mood for jokes right now," Hank said.

"How well did you really know her?" Morgan asked as he poured them each a finger. Hank took his glass but didn't immediately drink from it.

"Well enough to like Jasmine. Well enough to believe she had a future in my field. Not well enough to know much about her personal life."

"But that's still well enough to call her a friend." Morgan raised his glass. Hank followed suit and clinked them together.

"Yes, it is," Hank said. "To Jasmine." After they both took a drink, Morgan poured himself some more while Hank set his glass aside.

"I promise to take good care of her body until we can get her back to the States," Morgan said.

"I know you will. Is this the first time you've had someone die on you in the middle of an expedition?"

"No. I had one botanist that hired me who got stung by a wasp. Apparently, it was the first time in his life that he'd ever been stung, so he didn't realize he was allergic. We had the medical supplies for him, but he still ended up dying from complications. I liked the guy. That was a terrible thing, but nothing even close to what we saw today."

Hank shook his head. "I'm still trying to wrap my head around it. It doesn't even seem real. What we saw shouldn't have been possible."

"Hank, I've been working as a captain ferrying people like you up and down the Amazon River since you were in high school. A lot has changed in that time. It's not nearly as wild as it once was, but there's still shit down here that even seasoned scientists like yourself would have trouble explaining. Stop saying that what we saw wasn't possible. That snake was there. It was real. So obviously it *is* possible. Instead of denying that, put that over-sized brain of yours to work and start figuring out what any of this means."

"It's just... I would need more data," Hank said. "What we've got to go on is practically nothing."

"Then what would you need to get more data?" Morgan asked.

Hank snorted. "Another encounter with the *Titanoboa*."

"Sorry, professor, but if it's all the same to you, I'd rather avoid that." He tipped back the rest of his rum. Despite the situation, Hank couldn't help but smile.

"So, uh, whatever happened to you only drinking whiskey? Last I checked, you were still refusing to drink rum because of the jokes about your name."

"I do only drink whiskey, but only in front of people I don't trust. Truth is, I hate whiskey. I like rum so much better, but I'll drink it in front of people that I know won't make the same tired jokes."

"And if I made those jokes now?"

"You won't. That's the kind of guy you are, and that's why I'm okay with the forbidden drink in front of you. I also trust you to not tell anyone that you saw me doing this, you understand?"

"I understand completely."

"It's just about time for everyone to switch shifts," Morgan said. "Although, if you want, I can make sure there's a half hour of just you and your girl alone below decks, if that's what you want."

"No, we already agreed we weren't going to do anything like that on this trip," Hank said. "That's not what this is about yet."

"Then when will it be about that?" Morgan asked.

"I don't know. After I retire from this kind of thing?"

"So you're actually serious about this being your last

expedition in the field? I'm telling you this right away, if that douchebag Randy actually takes your place doing this, he's going to have to find another captain to help him."

"I get the impression he doesn't even realize he needs anyone experienced with him in the field. He's under the delusion that his money means he doesn't need to do any work," Hank said. "He won't last long. You won't have to worry about him."

"No, I don't think I will. Your girl is more likely to take your place than him."

"You think so?"

"I told you, I've led a lot of people down this river. I know the right look when I see it. She'll be back. It's getting into her blood. I suppose it's just a question of whether you'll be back with her."

Hank finished off what little was left in his glass. "And I suppose you'll still be here?"

"I'll be on the Amazon River until the day I'm gone. I fully intend to die in it, if possible."

"Just not soon," Hank said, his tone going from jovial to dark as he thought about Jasmine.

"No, not soon," Morgan said.

Hank stumbled off to his bunk, fully intending not to wake until the morning.

That plan didn't work out.

7

With as much time as Hank had spent with Morgan on the Amazon, an interesting pattern had taken hold of him when it came to sleep. Whenever his body felt the subtle rocking of the boat beneath him, he would wake periodically, although not fully, as though he was checking to make sure that everything was okay without actually doing it consciously. It was during one of these brief moments of wakefulness that he realized there was some kind of commotion on the deck. He instantly came fully awake, called out to anyone else in the bunks that something was going on, and then immediately ran up to the deck. There, he found Stu, the captain, and Erin shining a searchlight out onto the water.

"What's going on?" Hank asked as Katherine and Randy came up behind them, each of them rubbing the sleep from their eyes. Neither of them seemed to notice the tone of alarm among the rest of the crew yet.

"I saw something out on the water," Stu said.

"Is it the *Titanoboa*?" Hank asked. If it was, then they had a problem. Morgan was shining the light in front of them, not behind, which meant that the giant snake would have somehow found a way around them without triggering the sonar. But Morgan shook his head.

"The sonar suggests something smaller but in a large group."

"Any chance that it's something we don't actually need to worry about?" Randy asked.

"Maybe," Morgan said. "There's lots of things about that size that live in the Amazon River but don't actually pose a threat. The majority of creatures out there just want to mind their own business."

"But I could have sworn there was a section of the water out there that was in a frenzy," Stu said. "You're not going to find dolphins acting like that, I assume."

Actually, Hank thought river dolphins might, but he wasn't going to say anything. Given what had happened that day, it would be better for them to assume the possibility of danger rather than that everything would just happen to be okay.

"How long ago did you see it?" Hank asked.

"It was about a minute ago," Stu said. "I don't know. Maybe it was nothing. I'm getting tired. It could just be a trick of the…"

"Wait, there!" Morgan said, pointing out at the blackened water far ahead and to the left of them. He quickly turned the spotlight to face that direction, and this time, they all saw it. The way the water bubbled and boiled with activity was distinctly different than what they had seen with the *Titanoboa*, but it was not completely unfamiliar to Hank. Nor, he guessed, was it new to Morgan. They turned to look at each other, both of them saying their thought at the same time.

"Piranhas."

Randy held his hands up in the air. "Wait, wait, wait. I thought you said piranhas wouldn't show up until we were much farther down the river than this? And that even if they did, they wouldn't be a problem?"

"Just because they're active doesn't mean that we have any evidence that they're a problem," Katherine said.

"And as far as their location goes, we already have evidence that the local ecology has been disrupted," Hank said. "The presence of the *Titanoboa* might have changed food distribution, which in turn might have changed when and where the piranhas hunt."

"So, does that mean they're not going to provide a problem?" Erin asked.

"I guess we're about to find out," Morgan said. He moved the searchlight to follow the churning trail of the carnivorous fish. "It looks like they're approaching us."

While Hank normally wouldn't have been alarmed by any of this, he noticed something unexpected as they got closer to the *Lucky Lucy*, and some of the fish were physically visible to those in the boat. The average piranha shouldn't have been much bigger than his hand. Each of these, however, was roughly the size of a basketball.

"Piranhas aren't my specialty, but those certainly seem to be larger than average."

"They're not my specialty either, unless you count when I roast them with a fine garlic sauce," Morgan said. "But you are correct. Piranhas aren't supposed to get that big."

Hank had to back away from the edge of the boat as one of the piranhas got close, jumping and snapping at him in midair. While piranhas weren't within his biological area of expertise, he had seen enough of them in his travels to know there were a few things different about this one's shape. Most notably, their jaws were larger with sharper teeth. These were more like what the general public believed piranhas to be than what they actually were.

While Erin kept a healthy distance away from the edge of the boat, she scooted closer to the side than any of the others would dare with the huge carnivorous fish patrolling the water around them. "We should be safe as long as we stay on the boat, right?" she asked. "Piranhas don't pose a threat to anything outside of the water?"

The boat rocked as something thudded against the hull just below the water.

"When they're normal sized? Maybe not," Hank said. "When they're the size of a watermelon? We might have a problem."

"Is there anything we can do to distract them?" Stu asked. "Like, throw some meat in the water away from the boat?"

"Maybe," Morgan said. "I have some slabs of beef that I keep in the freezer to act as bait in situations just like this. For these things, though, we're going to need the biggest chunks I have. Randy, do you want to come and help me?"

"Uh, I don't know if I should be lifting anything heavy. I have a bad back, and…"

"Oh, for crap's sake," Katherine said. "If you're not man enough to carry heavy things, then I'll do it."

Katherine followed Morgan below deck while everyone else stayed near the edge and watched the bizarre display below them. "First an impossible snake, now impossible piranhas," Hank muttered. "Normally, I'd be careful about making connections where there isn't enough evidence…"

"…but this is just way too much to be a coincidence," Erin finished. "If the *Titanoboa* is some kind of throwback to an extinct species, do you think these might be the same thing?"

"Could be, but like I said, I don't know enough about fish or paleontology to be sure. It's too bad we can't get some kind of sample."

"What, are you saying you'd like to catch one?" Stu asked.

"More or less," Hank said. "Catching the *Titanoboa* for further scientific study isn't going to be possible, at least not right now with the meager equipment we have. But catching one of these? Even with their size, there might be something we can do."

"Can we please not?" Randy asked. "I see way too many ways in which this can go wrong."

Everyone else completely ignored Randy. "I know that I saw a heavy-duty fishing net among the captain's equipment," Erin said. "Hold on. I think I know where it is."

Erin returned with the net much faster than Morgan and Katherine did with the meat. Hank took the net from her and inspected it, trying to judge whether or not it would work in this situation. The design resembled a normal commercial fishing net that Hank might be able to find by walking into a department store, but it had obviously been designed with much sturdier and rambunctious fish in mind than what one might find on a weekend fishing trip at the lake. The handle was longer and made of some kind of polycarbonate that Hank was unfamiliar with, while the net itself, rather than being weaved from nylon or some other similar material, looked to be made from steel cables. The rugged construction of the net made sense, give the rather dangerous things Captain Morgan might need to use it on in the Amazon River, and Hank was satisfied that it would be enough to hold even one of these ridiculous-sized piranhas.

"Let's at least do this safely," Hank said. "The handle is long enough that all of us can hold onto it. I'll take the front and we'll try to scoop one up, but stay away from the edge. This may be a big scientific find, but it's not worth the risk of anyone falling in."

Hank took the front, with Erin in the middle and Stu holding the back end of the pole. Hank tried to get Randy to take a spot in between Erin and Stu, but he absolutely refused to even get that close to the water. Carefully, Hank lowered the end of the net into the mass of fish shifting and churning at the side of the boat. To his surprise, though, even with the mass of piranhas as thick as it was, he couldn't get anything into the net.

"They keep getting close to the net, but they swim out just when I'm about to scoop one up," Hank said. "It's almost like they're too smart to get caught that way."

"Is that possible?" Erin asked.

"Who knows?" Hank said.

"Jesus Christ, Hank, seriously?" The voice came from back in the direction of the cabin, and Hank looked back to see both Morgan and Katherine struggling to carry sides of beef. Ironically, despite being the seasoned river man with plenty of experience hauling around heavy loads, Katherine seemed to be the one having the easier time with the huge chunk of meat.

"Morgan, it would really be advantageous if we…"

The captain cut Hank off before he could finish. "I know exactly what you're trying to do. And I don't care what your scientist instincts say you should do. My captain's instincts say get the hell away from the killer fish."

While Hank had managed to win arguments with Morgan in the past, he knew better than to even try when the captain thought safety was at risk. Reluctantly, Hank pulled the net out of the water and, after the captain had set down his piece of meat, handed it to Morgan.

"Right," Morgan said. "What we're going to do is throw the meat into the water at the stern, and then we're going to accelerate as fast as –"

Something rammed into the *Lucky Lucy* again, this time with more force than the first time the piranhas had attacked. Morgan, almost losing his balance, reacted by trying to steady himself. Unfortunately, with the net still in hand, he accidentally hit Stu in the chest in the process. Stu stumbled backward, hit the railing, and then leaned precariously back over the side. Hank, moving quickly, grabbed Stu by the shirt and kept him from toppling.

Before any of them could celebrate the lucky grab, however, the boat shuddered again. Hank's hand slipped through Stu's shirt, and down he went.

"Stu!" Katherine screamed.

Most of the others weren't close enough to the edge to see

what happened next, considering how fast it happened, but Hank had a front row seat to the whole gory show. There was a colossal splash, and before Stu's head could even come back to the surface, the water around where he had gone in turned red with his blood.

"Do it!" Morgan screamed. "Throw the meat over the far side! Lure the piranhas away from him!"

Hank could hear chaos behind him as the others ran to follow the captain's commands, but he knew that it had already been too late the instant Stu hit the water. One of his hands came up, as though trying to reach for help, but there were already large chunks of skin and muscle missing. It looked like a corpse trying to reach up out of its grave.

Hank heard two splashes from the other side of the boat, the sounds of the meat going into the water, and the piranhas dashed away to the other side, but there was little more than picked-apart bones sinking below the dark water to mark the place where Stu had previously been.

With Katherine still screaming for Stu, the boat began to race on ahead, the captain desperate to get them away from the murderous fish.

8

Morgan kept the *Lucky Lucy* going as fast as he could until the first light of morning started to sparkle on the calm river. It was a calmness that Hank didn't entirely trust, given everything he had seen lurking below the water over the last twenty-four hours, but he still allowed himself to hope that the still waters meant they were out of range of the school of mutant piranhas. If they weren't, then that meant going anywhere near the water might not be safe.

Out of all of them, Katherine was obviously the one who took Stu's death the hardest. But instead of immediately crying, she had shut down and simply stared vacantly ahead of her, barely blinking the whole time. Hank couldn't even be sure if she was awake or doing some kind of weird thing where she slept with her eyes open. Randy was also in shock, but for him, it mostly manifested in a fear of going anywhere near the edge of the boat. Erin seemed to be holding it together the best out of all of them, doing her best to comfort Katherine and stay active in helping with the running of the boat, now that the only person other than the captain with any real nautical experience was gone.

To Hank's surprise, Captain Morgan seemed to be taking it just as hard as anyone else. Although he tried to hide it, Hank could almost swear that he saw the gruff, burly man hiding tears on occasion. In all likelihood, he probably blamed himself for what had happened to Stu. He'd been the one that had hit Stu with the net pole, after all. Then again, maybe it was just that, despite everything he said and did and how he acted, Captain M. Morgan really did care about every single person that set foot on his boat. For the brief time they were there, they were his crew, and to men like Morgan, a crew might as well have been family.

With day on them again, Hank had a better idea of where exactly they were on the river. While a light rain had started to fall, the Amazon was still vibrant and alive with life at the height of the wet season. The shore that would have marked the edge of the river during drier times was non-existent in quite a few places, giving the edge a swampy look where the trees appeared to grow out of the river itself. Unidentified creatures called out from deep within the thick jungle, and a subtle haze just over the water gave the entire scene a dream-like quality. In this setting, it was almost possible to forget that they had lost two members of their crew within the last day, and any freakish beasts that might be following them seemed hundreds of miles away.

The surreal atmosphere was so complete that Hank almost didn't believe his own eyes when a large, boxy shape started to form at the distance of his vision. He had to blink several times before he could admit that he wasn't seeing things. There was indeed some kind of man-made structure tangled within the exposed roots of the floodplain trees.

"Hey, does anyone else see that?" Hank called out. At his words, Morgan and Erin joined him out on the wet deck. Katherine was in her bunk below, still in shock, while Randy refused to leave the cabin at the moment.

Morgan went back into the cabin just long enough to get some binoculars, but by the time he returned, the *Lucky Lucy* had drawn close enough they didn't even need any aid to know the structure was a boat. It was roughly the same size as the *Lucky Lucy*, if perhaps slightly smaller, and didn't look like it had been marooned in the floodplain for very long.

"What do you think?" Hank asked. "Should we go check it out?"

"There's no question that we're going to," Morgan said. "If there's anyone there in distress, it's part of my code to go help them. And if there isn't anyone there, then it's salvage. There might be things on there that can help us."

Morgan anchored the *Lucky Lucy*, then bid Erin to keep an eye on things. He and Hank would go out to the stranded boat in one of Morgan's emergency rowboats, considering there was no way anything larger could get through the trees in the flooded area without suffering the same fate. The two of them set out, mindful all the while of the new perils from yesterday that could be lurking below them at any moment.

The boat was mostly intact, even if it was completely incapable of going back out on the water without some major patch jobs. As Morgan rowed them closer to it, Hank could see several holes in the hull that might have been consistent with what they'd recently seen the abnormally large piranhas do. While there were no signs of anyone still on it, some of the gear webbed down on the deck suggested the boat's previous owner had been well-supplied.

"You see that?" Morgan asked. "Gas cans. If we're lucky, they're still full and we'll have enough to get somewhere where we can get help."

Once they were almost on top of it, Hank could see the scarred-up paint job of a name on the side of the boat. *Scarman's Chance*.

"I know that name," Morgan muttered. "The *Scarman's Chance* was doing supply runs for some scientist camped somewhere in the Amazon. Except I haven't heard anything about it for the last three weeks. I thought they'd set up shop much farther down the river, but…apparently not."

The closer they got to the wrecked boat, the more evident it became that no one living had been on it for those missing three weeks. Hank kept expecting to see skeletons in the water, picked clean by the unnatural piranhas, but there was no sign of any human being at all.

"Careful not to get in the water when we climb aboard it," Morgan said. "There may not be any sign of those piranhas at the moment, but they were obviously around here at some point."

Morgan tied off the rowboat, then led the way climbing up the ripped-up side of the *Scarman's Chance*. Once they were both on the deck, which was at an unnatural angle thanks to the way the boat had come to rest among the submerged tree roots, Morgan went straight for the canisters he had assumed were full of gas. Hank, with no special destination on the boat in mind, started to wander around in search of clues as to what might have happened here. There was debris littered all around the deck and evidence in several places that the crew had been in the middle of other things when whatever tragedy had happened. And Hank didn't doubt that it was indeed a tragedy, as several spots near the stern were splashed with dried blood. Shuddering, Hank avoided that for now. Whatever had gone on, there had to be clues elsewhere that wouldn't involve him having to make a closer inspection of the place where someone had likely died.

Below deck, in the captain's quarters, he thought he found what they were looking for. He called back up to the captain. "Hey, Morgan. You better come on down here and take a look at this."

When Morgan joined him, Hank led him to the captain's desk, which was strewn with a variety of papers. Many of them were damp from the weather, and a composition book that had probably served as the captain's log was so drenched that all the ink inside had run and made it unreadable. There were other things on the desk, though, that were still in good enough shape to tell them a story.

"There's a specific spot marked out on these maps," Morgan said. "An island in the middle of the river."

"Do you know it?" Hank asked.

"Yeah, not that I've ever stopped there. During the wet season, a large portion of the outer areas is under water, so it's not a particularly great spot to do anything at all, but now that I think about it, I have heard some rumors about someone setting up camp there."

"There's copies of receipts here, too," Hank said. "It looks like the *Scarman's Chance* was hired to transport a large number of supplies out to this island over the last nine months."

Morgan took a closer look at the smeared, handwritten receipts. "I can't quite make out the name of the person they were supposed to be delivering to. Uh, Sampson, maybe? Sanderson? No, wait. I think that's supposed to be a T. Sanderton."

"Wait," Hank said. "Sanderton? That wouldn't happen to be Dr. Annalisa Sanderton, would it?"

"Mmm, could be. Yeah, that seems like it could be the name written here. Why? Is that someone you know?"

"I should say so. Dr. Sanderton is a genius in the emerging field of paleo-genetics. I met her at a few conferences here or there. Her work and theories were brilliant. She was a bit shy and squirrelly, but then again, quite a few scientists are like that."

"Paleo-genetics? What the hell is that?"

"Exactly what it sounds like: the combination of the fields of paleontology and genetics. Dr. Sanderton was amassing one of the largest libraries of partially genetic codes for extinct creatures, and she..." Hank trailed off as he started to realize the implications of what he was saying.

"What? What is it?" Morgan asked.

"Can I see those receipts again?" Hank asked. Morgan handed them over, allowing Hank to pour over them, trying to get a better idea of what exactly had been shipped out to Dr. Sanderton's mysterious camp in the middle of the Amazon River Basin.

"Would you mind telling me what you're seeing there that my tiny brain can't, oh mighty professor?" Morgan asked sardonically.

"It's a, um, a theory, but that can't be right. Sanderton would never be involved in this kind of thing."

"Are you thinking maybe that she's somehow responsible for the *Titanoboa* and the weird piranhas?" Morgan asked.

"No. No, not at all. It's just..." He didn't finish. It was just that, while it was unlikely, he did see how someone with a highly active imagination could think that the equipment Sanderton had in her possession could be used for certain cloning experiments, and how that cloning could be used to bring certain extinct creatures back to life.

And yet that was all ridiculous. The science of these kinds of things had advanced quite a bit in recent years, but not by *that* much.

Right?

"Maybe this is something we can discuss another time," Morgan said. He rolled up the maps and stuffed them into a canvas pack to keep them from getting even further damaged in the increasing rain outside. "Right now, we need to get back to the *Lucky Lucy*."

"But we haven't even done a full search of everything," Hank said.

"As much as I would like to, my job as the guide you hired to get you up and down the Amazon is to keep you safe. And in case you haven't noticed, so far this time I've done a pretty shitty job of it."

"Morgan, you're not to blame for what's happened."

"Maybe I don't hold any real blame for your teaching assistant, but that kid last night? Hitting him was an accident, sure, but it was a rookie accident."

"If anyone is to blame for Stu's death, it's me," Hank said. "If I hadn't been trying to get one of those fish as a sample…"

"You were being as safe as you could be under the circumstances. But in the end, the buck stops here. Every death on the *Lucky Lucy* ultimately comes back to the captain. I've already got two deaths on this trip that I have to answer for. And in case you forgot, there's blood up on the deck and holes in this boat. Something came and killed the crew. Maybe it's gone, but maybe it's still here. Either way, sticking around is a bad idea."

"Okay, fine then. Let's go back up to the deck, load some of those gas cans onto the rowboat, and then –"

"Yeah, there's a problem with that," Morgan said. "They're empty. It looks more like they were hauling the empty cans away from somewhere."

"Possibly from that camp we saw on the maps?"

"Could be. Who knows. But there's nothing on this boat that's going to be able to help us. So it's time to move."

Hank followed Morgan back to the rowboat, and from there back to the *Lucky Lucy*. He wasn't sure, however, that they hadn't found anything that would help them. They had the maps now, as well as a name.

Sanderton. Hank just hoped Sanderton wasn't up to the possibly unethical atrocities he thought she could be doing.

9

Once they were back on the *Lucky Lucy*, Morgan and Hank explained everything they'd seen to the others. The captain laid out the maps in the cabin for everyone else to see, but he wasn't as interested now in Sanderton's secret camp so much as he was in something else he'd seen.

"Right there," Morgan said as he pointed at a mark the captain of the *Scarman's Chance* had made on a spot some distance inland. "The Amazon isn't as wild as it used to be, and large parts of it are being maintained by various park services or world-wide conservation organizations. There's a small station run by the World Wildlife Federation at the edge of some land they're monitoring. We can get help there."

Katherine stared at the map blankly, while Randy didn't seem to understand much of what he was seeing. Erin was the one who had to point out the problem with Morgan's idea. "If I'm reading the scale on the map correctly, that's at least a two-day's journey over land before we reach them. Wouldn't there be other ways that are easier and safer for us?"

"Sure, plenty," Morgan said. "Under normal circumstances. Except we're not dealing with normal circumstances, are we? We're low on fuel, so going too far down river is out of the question, and we've got freaky creatures behind us that turn any attempt to get back to where we started into a hellish gauntlet."

"Um, so you're saying there's nothing in the rainforest that would try eating us?" Randy asked.

"Maybe there are," Morgan said. "But anything like that in the forest are the creatures that are actually supposed to be there, not giant killer fish and prehistoric monsters. I don't know about you, but I certainly like my chances better going up against things that are actually supposed to be part of the normal order."

"And is this a play you agree with?" Erin asked Hank.

Hank couldn't answer right away. He had no doubt that the station Morgan wanted to head to would be able to help them, but he still wasn't sure if he wanted to discount the idea of heading to Dr. Sanderton's secret camp. Regardless of whether or not she had anything to do with what was happening (and that idea still seemed thoroughly ridiculous), the spot on the map that marked her hideaway was simply closer. Going by boat, they could be there by the end of the day. While Hank had no problem with the idea of hiking overland, he wasn't so sure that Erin, Randy, or Katherine were conditioned enough for that kind of grueling slog.

Morgan interrupted before he could say anything. "The professor here might be in charge of the scientific portions of the expedition, but I'm the one in charge of anything else. The truth is, there's no easy path here anymore."

"You make this all sound very ominous," Randy said. "It's almost like you're expecting more of us to die."

Katherine choked back a sob at that. Erin smacked Randy in the arm for the insensitive remark.

"Expecting? No," Morgan said. "But I do recognize that this entire thing has gone completely off the rails. The Amazon has always been a place for the unexpected, but this is light-years beyond. A different situation calls for different thinking. So are you all going to follow me to this WWF station, or are you going to try sticking around on the boat?"

It wasn't really a question, and they all knew it. While Hank knew his way around the Amazon and both Erin and Katherine had enough knowledge to take care of themselves, it was their captain who was really the one with the best chance at keeping them alive, even when faced with things Morgan himself couldn't fight against.

They anchored the *Lucky Lucy* just beyond the floodplain trees, made sure the boat was as secure as possible (including putting Jasmine's body in the place of the two meat slabs that had recently vacated the freezer, since they had every intention of coming back for her body and giving their deceased teammates a proper funeral), then went in to dry land by way of two rowboats. With the rain still gushing down on them, the group started what they were sure would be a very long and arduous journey on foot.

Morgan's machete slashed through the majority of the underbrush, but in some places, it was so thick that nothing they could do would rip through it. They had to take the long paths around these spots, sometimes adding nearly five minutes onto their journey just to go roughly twenty feet.

"I don't know if I'm going to be able to get very far like this," Katherine said. Her cheeks were still puffy with tears, and occasionally as they walked, Hank could hear her sniffle. Hank wasn't sure exactly how close she had been to Stu, but from her reaction, he could guess that they were more than just a hookup. Hank wanted to go over and comfort her, but he wasn't sure how. Erin, however, didn't seem to have the same problem, and she left Hank's side as they walked so she could gently touch Katherine on the arm.

"We're going to make it," Erin said to her. Katherine allowed herself a small, humorless smile, then hugged Erin before continuing on behind Morgan. As she did, Randy fell back in the line so that he was next to Hank.

"Save it, Randy. I'm not in the mood," Hank said.

"Actually, I was thinking that maybe I should apologize to you," Randy said.

Hank opened his mouth to respond, then closed it again when he realized he didn't have the slightest clue what to say.

"I know you think I don't know the first thing about herpetology or anything the Folger Institute does, and the truth is, you're right. I actually don't want anything to do with any of this."

"I, uh, wait. Then why the hell are you even here? I was under the impression that you were trying to push me out just so that you could take my place as the Folger Institute's main field man."

"Hank, seriously? I certainly have my opinions about you and the way you do things, but you're on the verge of retirement. You've made that abundantly clear. Why would I need to do anything dastardly to get you out of the way?"

"In that case, I'm confused."

"The only reason I'm involved in the Folger Institute at all is because my family pressured me into it," Randy said.

"Okay, that's a new one," Hank said. "Most of the time parents will pressure their children into being doctors or lawyers or going to business school. This is the first time I've ever heard of someone being forced into the family business of staring at lizards and frogs. I suppose you really want to be a musician. Isn't that the stereotype?"

"Oh hell no. You actually had it right, only backward. I want to go to business school. All this brainy science crap? I won't ever be able to make heads or tails of it. You can keep your Panama hats and machetes in the underbrush and adventure at the far ends of the Earth. I want to wear a suit and tie and sit behind a desk. That's all I've ever wanted to do since I was a kid."

"Huh." Hank had to pause for a long time to digest all this

before he could say anything else in response. "Apology accepted then, I guess."

By this time, Erin had finished whatever it was she felt she needed to do to soothe Katherine. Only about forty minutes had passed since they'd left the boat, but Hank already felt his body protesting the hike and the constant drenching from above. He almost wanted to ask Morgan if they could take a break, and he was sure Morgan would allow it for him, but they had far too long to go, and they couldn't keep taking breaks every time the old man got a little winded.

Erin nudged him by the shoulder. "Hey, you okay?"

"Fine," Hank said. Erin would have had to be deaf not to hear the exhausted wheeze in his voice.

"You're being obstinate. Come on, just ask Morgan for a break."

They stopped, silently letting the other three pull ahead. If Morgan noticed two of his group had fallen behind, he apparently thought they were okay to take care of themselves for a moment. Or else he was so focused on his duty of getting his charges to safety that he was actually letting safety slide.

"Hey, what's even going on?" Erin asked. "So, yeah, you've got a few years on you, but you're normally not like this. You're, you know, energetic, if you know what I mean."

"Erin, this isn't the time for innuendo. Two people are dead."

"Yeah, I know. You think I don't? But we're not. And if we want to keep it that way, we both need to keep our heads above the piranha-infested water, so to speak."

"If we get out of this…"

"We are, Hank."

"If we do, I think I've made my decision. I really am done in the field."

"Oh."

Somehow she managed to get a whole lot of meaning and

feeling into those two letters. "Oh what?" he asked.

"I was just thinking it was time for me to embrace fieldwork more. As in, once I'm finished with my degree, this is what I want to do with it."

Hank nodded, suddenly understanding. Their relationship was hard enough as it was with just the age gap. His time in the field hadn't helped, which was part of the reason they had wanted to do this one together. But if he was done and she was just starting, that meant there wasn't a lot of hope for them to have a future.

"You know what? This isn't the right place to have this conversation," Hank said.

"Right," Erin said. She wouldn't look him in the eye. "We'll continue this somewhere that's dry and where there aren't strange prehistoric creatures floating around in the…"

She stopped.

"What?" Hank asked. "What is it?"

"I thought I heard a hiss."

Hank's first thought was that it could have been anything. They were in the rainforest, after all, and the Amazon wasn't exactly short on snakes that could be coiling down from the trees at any moment and hissing right in their ears. But as Hank heard it too, he knew damned well that this wasn't some normal tree snake.

The sound was coming from behind them in the direction of the river. And as the noise got louder, it became obvious that it was attached to something very, very large.

The *Titanoboa* was back.

10

The two of them ran.

Unfortunately, at some point, the two of them had completely lost track of their three companions. Also, to their misfortune, they had somehow lost the path that Morgan had been cutting through the jungle with his machete. They weren't even running for a minute when Erin tripped over something and fell hard to the ground, letting out a small scream of pain as her ribs fell right into a rotting log. One look at her face told Hank that, if she hadn't broken a rib, then she had at least bruised something that was not going to make walking or breathing easy for her.

"Nnnnnn!" Erin said as she tried to keep her agony silent. Then, "Hank, I can hear it. I think it's right behind us."

Hank pulled her aside deep into a copse of bromeliads in the hope that the smell would hide their presence. From their vantage point, they had a perfect view as the *Titanoboa* showed itself again.

The fleeting glimpses Hank had gotten of it in the water were impressive, but they were nothing compared to the impression it marked on his psyche as the monster snake slithered onto the path where they had just been. The thing's head alone was about as long as Hank's torso. Its scales were a pale gray with rust-red stripes. On something smaller, Hank would have seen that kind of coloring and figured that the snake was likely not venomous, but at that size, venom was not what they would need to worry about. A snake like this would more likely hunt by quickly wrapping itself around its prey and then crushing it to death before then swallowing its meal whole. At its thickest point, the *Titanoboa*'s body was about as wide as a small pony would be tall. The creature could very easily fit two or three whole humans inside its stomach and still have plenty of room to spare.

Hank put a hand over Erin's mouth in the hope that he could keep the *Titanoboa* from hearing her whimpers of pain, not that he thought it would do much good if the snake truly decided to target them. The monster's tongue flicked in a different direction, though, and it slithered toward some other scent that it had picked up. The enormous ropey body seemed to slide past them for an abnormally long time before it was finally away.

"It's headed inland," Hank whispered in her ear. "We should head the opposite direction."

"We can't just leave the others," Erin whispered back. "We've got to find some way to warn Randy, Katherine, and the captain that it's coming."

While Hank knew that any such attempt would be folly, he knew he wouldn't be able to live with himself if something happened to the others and he had failed to try helping. Trying to follow or get around the snake on foot, however, would be suicide. He looked up at the tree next to them, noting all the knots and branches they could use as handholds to climb it. "Do you think you're okay to try getting up there?" he asked.

Erin tentatively poked her bruised ribs, then shrugged. "If that's really what we have to do."

"It's what you have to do," Hank said. "You're not going to

be able to run, so you'll have to get up in the tree a safe distance while I…"

"Uh-uh. None of that Mr. Chivalry garbage," Erin said. "No offense, but as you keep saying when you try to make excuses about us not being together, you're old enough to be my grandpa. Even when I'm hurt, we're going to be just about even as far as following the giant dino snake trying to find our friends."

"Huh. Erin, I'm not sure whether to be insulted by any of that or proud of you."

Erin flashed him a hundred-watt smile that somehow managed to shine through the accumulated dirt on her face. "How about both? Now let's get moving."

The *Titanoboa* had left a very clear trail of broken vines, branches, and crushed underbrush for them to follow. While Hank was the one with more field experience between the two of them, Erin proved to be a natural at moving silently in pursuit of their prey, her small body able to squeeze through gaps and duck under tangled, low-hanging vines with an ease that Hank had never managed even in his prime.

Hank saw something in the path ahead of them, causing him to grab Erin before she could continue charging headlong into the jungle. Before she could ask what he was doing, he held a single finger up to his mouth to signal quiet, then pointed at what he had seen. The tip of the *Titanoboa*'s tale was poking out through the brush up ahead. The snake had stopped, although the monster was so long and the forest so thick that they couldn't what might have caused it to stop.

Erin leaned in extremely close to whisper in his ear. "We've got to get around it." Under any other circumstances, Hank would have disagreed vehemently. The last thing they would want to do is get on the business end of a creature capable of consuming a whole human in one gulp. It was possible, though, that the snake had targeted their friends and was merely waiting for the proper moment to strike. Hank nodded, then indicated a path through the vines and bushes that he hoped would allow them to get ahead and warn the others in time.

Before they could move, however, the tip of the tail vanished into the leaves, and somewhere beyond there was an ear-piercing scream.

Hank recognized the voice as Katherine's, at least up until the moment when it abruptly cut off.

Although it still would have been most prudent find a safer path around, his instincts took over and he ran directly toward the scream of his student. Erin was right behind him. He would have expected her to protest that running directly into danger wasn't the smart thing to do, but she said nothing. Instead, the two of them, both with their second wind now, burst through the brush into a clearing where the unfortunate scene was already playing out.

In the second or two Hank had to assess the situation, he guessed that Morgan, Randy, and Katherine had probably finally taken notice that two of their members were missing, and had likely been in the process of setting up a plan to go back and find them. The clearing had provided the perfect spot for them to stage this rescue effort, yet at the same time, it had been the ideal spot for the *Titanoboa* to ambush them. Randy was sprawled out on the ground, having either fallen or been knocked over as the monster snake had attacked, and he was currently gaping up at the horrifying sight in front of him with a slack jaw. Morgan had his machete in hand, his body tensed in a defensive position in case the *Titanoboa* forgot about its current target and came after him.

But the worst part of all was Katherine.

Hank and Erin stopped, both of them staring up with utter horror at the grisly tableau before them. The snake was reared up, towering above them all, with its massive trunk coiled around a small, struggling creature in the center. If it hadn't been for the scream they'd heard, Hank might not have even recognized the *Titanoboa*'s victim as Katherine at all. Its thick, sinewy body had already crushed her, making her look like a small broken doll being waved around by a petulant child. Her face was purple from lack of oxygen, and her limbs waved drunkenly and bonelessly. In the few brief seconds since its initial attack, the snake had already broken practically every bone in her body, and it was immediately evident that, even if the snake let her go now, she would die soon after from her gruesome injuries.

All of this made it somehow worse that she wasn't dead yet. Hank could still see the slight movement in her chest as she tried to breathe through a crushed rib cage. Her jaw continued to work as though she still wanted to scream, but she couldn't even get enough air to make the noise.

Morgan saw Hank and Erin come into the clearing, causing him to break his paralysis. He roughly manhandled Randy back to his feet, then pulled him in their direction. "Go!" Morgan screamed at them. "Run!"

"We can't just leave Katherine behind!" Erin yelled back at him. Morgan didn't respond, instead racing past them and chopping at the vines with his machete in an effort to get them away faster. After some hesitation, Erin followed. Whether she'd seen it or not, on some level, she must have known that there was no longer any chance for Katherine, but as long as the snake was distracted with her, the rest of them still had a fighting chance to live.

Hank, however, was ever the herpetologist. He stayed back to help steady Randy on his feet, but deep down he knew the real reason he was so hesitant to leave. He'd studied reptiles and amphibians his whole life, so he knew what it looked like when a snake fed, but his morbid curiosity insisted that he didn't know what it looked like when *this* snake fed. And so, despite the horror of what the *Titanoboa*'s meal consisted of, he couldn't keep himself from watching Katherine's end.

The *Titanoboa* opened its mouth, distended its jaw, then slowly lowered its maw over Katherine's head. Katherine continued to struggle for a moment, but the mouth must have cut off what little air she was still able to get into her lungs. As her body fell completely still, the coils that had been crushing and holding her came undone, allowing the snake to work its way down her body by degrees. Every few seconds, it would push forward again, first covering her neck, then her shoulders. Her breasts, already horribly misshapen from what the *Titanoboa* had done to her, squeezed together tight as they fit under the snake's lip. It appeared to be able to move faster after that, crossing her stomach and taking in her hips, until only her legs were still sticking out. Her feet twitched, although at that point it was likely from some kind of aftershock in her nerves rather than an honest attempt for her to struggle.

The *Titanoboa* lifted its head up and back, providing a clear path for the girl's body to slide down into oblivion. Hank could see a vague outline of Katherine in the monster's throat. As her feet slipped in and the snake's jaw closed tight behind her, the bulge in the snake's throat gave one final twitch, as though Katherine had temporarily woken up and was trying to escape with her very last breath.

Then the shape was still. It slid down and vanished deep within the thicker portions of the snake, where Hank would not be able to tell that the young woman he had just recently been talking to was now on her way to being broken down into base nutrients.

Finally, Hank's paralysis broke, and he and Erin ran to join the others.

11

Once they were a safe distance and didn't hear any sign that the *Titanoboa* was immediately following them, they slowed down just enough to catch their breath and talk. Hank expected immediate recriminations from Morgan and Randy at his and Erin's absence, but they didn't say anything. That was fine, as Hank was more than capable of finding ways of blaming Katherine's death on himself. He already knew that Erin would try to tell him it wasn't their fault, that their falling behind hadn't had anything to do with the *Titanoboa* catching up to the others, and he supposed that eventually he might even believe it. But for now, the sense of guilt was intense, right along with the disgust and terror he still felt at the sight of his student getting eaten.

"Can we really afford to slow down?" Randy asked. "That thing's still behind us."

"The chances of it immediately following us aren't that large," Hank said. "Um, it's horrible to say, but, uh, the *Titanoboa* just ate. With something that size, it could probably eat a lot more, but it's not going to be in as big of a hurry, given how slow snakes digest their...their prey."

"Jesus," Erin muttered to herself. Her eyes were wide and

vacant, even while her words remained lucid. "Do we really have to talk about her that way? That prey had a name."

"And so do we," Morgan said. "If we want to keep those names instead of just becoming the second and third helpings, we need to be smart. Maybe we can slow down, but we can't stop." Morgan led them down the path they had previously taken, heading back to the river. Between the brush he cleared and the plant life the *Titanoboa* had crushed in its pursuit of them, the going back proved to be much easier.

"Where are we even heading?" Randy asked. "Do we have a plan?"

"Sure do," Morgan said. "The only option we seem to have left. We're going to try finding this Dr. Sanderton woman that was mentioned in the receipts and maps from the *Scarman's Chance*."

"Are we sure that's a good idea?" Erin asked. "Weren't we thinking that maybe this woman had something to do with the nightmare creatures we've been seeing?"

Morgan huffed and picked up his pace. The rest of them were forced to follow suit. "Look, it's really quite simple. We can't go back, and we can't try going over land anymore, not given how quickly that thing was able to follow us. If it got this far, it can only be chasing us, and we're running out of directions to run. The only option we have left is to keep going down the river, either until we find this woman that's supposedly behind this, or until we reach some settlement or group that can get us out of here."

"And if the maps we found on the *Scarman's Chance* are any indication," Erin said, "then this Sanderton woman shouldn't be too far ahead. She was, what, only about seven to ten more miles down?"

"And what exactly are we supposed to do if we run into her?" Randy asked. "Ask her politely if she's responsible for the giant mutant animals we've been running into?" "No, I refuse to believe she has anything to do with this," Hank said. "Her reputation used to be impeccable."

"Used to be?" Morgan asked.

Hank frowned. "Yeah, there's been some stories floating around that she was acting strange the last couple of times she was seen. Erratic behavior at the university she worked with, things like that." After contemplating it in silence for a couple of seconds, something occurred to him. "Now that I think of it, there were some stories that she'd been part of a World Health Organization investigation in Eastern Europe and Russia."

"I thought you said she was a paleo-geneticist," Erin said. "What would she be doing working with the WHO?"

"The permafrost in Siberia has been melting in recent years," Hank said. "Bacteria and viruses are being released that haven't been seen on Earth for as long as humans have been around. Several people that were involved with that project have recently been revealed to be infected with prions that have previously never been seen before."

"Uh, what the hell is a prion?" Randy asked.

"A prion is kind of similar to a virus, except, um, not," Erin said. "It's a misfolded protein. Unlike a virus or a bacterium, it can only enter a host by being consumed. Once in the body, it gets into the brain and attacks it."

"Wait, isn't that how Mad Cow Disease works?" Morgan asked.

"Yes, Mad Cow is in fact caused by prions. There are a number of different prion diseases recorded throughout the world, and there's been increasing speculation among the scientific community that this is exactly what was discovered during that project in Eastern Europe. And there's no cure for prion diseases. A couple of the people involved have died."

"And if she were infected with this, could that explain how

she might go from a respectable researcher to a mad scientist bringing back extinct monsters in the Amazon?" Morgan asked.

"Well, I guess it would depend entirely on the prion," Hank said. "If this new one is attacking parts of her brain responsible for morality and ethical reasoning, yet leaving alone a lot of her higher functions? Yeah, I suppose it's possible."

"Possible," Erin said. "But you still don't want to believe it?"

Only twenty minutes had passed since they'd run the other direction from the *Titanoboa*, but the Amazon River was already back in their view again. Rather than slowing down, they sped up until they were in the rowboats and paddling as fast as possible back to the *Lucky Lucy*. Once back on board, they brought up the anchor and continued on their way. Only then did they allow themselves another moment to breathe, and they all gathered in the cabin to discuss what was next.

"Just in case anyone thinks there's still a debate on this, I'm making an executive decision," Morgan said. "We're heading to the island of Dr. Sanderton."

"Sounds like an H.G. Wells novel," Erin muttered.

"And you really think that's wise?" Randy asked Morgan. "Because I sure as hell don't."

"You don't get to decide what's wise and what isn't," Morgan said. "I'm the captain."

"Yes, yes, so you keep reminding us," Randy said. "Our safety is your business and all that, blah, blah, blah. And gee, you've sure done a bang-up job at keeping us all safe so far. I'm sure that Jasmine, Stu, and Katherine would all give you five stars on Yelp, if they weren't, you know, dead."

Morgan reared up in Randy's face. To anyone who hadn't spent a lot of time with the captain, Hank was sure Morgan looked nothing but intimidating. Hank, however, could see just enough beyond the façade to realize that something in Randy's accusations had hit him hard. Whether he was trying to hide it or not, there would be a part of Morgan that absolutely believed he was in fact at fault for the three deaths so far.

"You need to shut up with that shit right now, kid," Morgan said. "If you don't, I'm going to –"

"How many times have you already threatened me on this trip?" Randy asked. "And yet you haven't done anything to me. You practically haven't done anything at all, except get a few good people killed."

"Oh stuff it, Randy," Erin said. "You didn't even know them. They were nothing to you. But I did. They were my friends. And I'm not going to let you use their deaths just so you can have an advantage in your own personal dick-measuring contest."

"Alright, that's enough, everyone!" Hank yelled. All bickering between the other three stopped. "We can't be at each other's throats like this and expect to live. The *Titanoboa* is still out there, and while it may need a break after its last, uh, meal, it's big enough to still be hungry. Not to mention the piranhas, as well as any other crazy creature that may be roaming around now that we haven't seen yet."

"You really think there's more?" Erin asked.

Hank took a deep breath and tried to calm down. "Whether or not Sanderton has anything to do with this, you have to admit that it can't possibly be a natural occurrence. Someone or something let creatures out into the wild that shouldn't be there anymore. If it were just the *Titanoboa*, I might think that was the main part of whatever this experiment is. But then if you add in the piranhas, you have to acknowledge how little the two creatures have in common. That suggests someone is doing this with a wide range of species. And a wide range of species implies more."

"Hank's right," Morgan said. He looked at Randy. "As much as I would like to continue tearing into you, you little weasel, we don't have the time for blaming each other. We're all still in danger. And even if we had anywhere we would be able to reach with as little fuel as we have left, I still don't see how we could ignore the clues that point to Sanderton's island."

"If she is the one behind this, we have to get proof," Erin said. "At the very least, we'd have to see what she's doing with our own eyes."

"And if she's not doing it, that would be valuable information as well," Hank said. "Not only could we cross a suspect off the list, but we'd have another expert that might be able to help us figure out what's going on."

"Well, I still think going anywhere near her is crazy," Randy said. "But it's not like we have any other options."

"Good. Then we all agree, not that it matters," Morgan said. "That's the direction we're going. If the *Lucky Lucy* goes at its fastest, we could be there somewhere under two hours."

Hank cringed. "Two hours might not be enough time to get a good head start on the *Titanoboa*."

"You really think it'll still be hungry?" Erin asked.

"I wish I could say for certain, but this is a creature that hasn't been witnessed alive on Earth for millions of years, and all we've had to study it is a few vertebrae. It's not like we have detailed data on its feeding patterns."

"If it comes after us in less than two hours, then we're just going to have to try being ready for it."

"Don't you have any weapons on board?" Randy asked.

Morgan responded simply by holding his machete.

"You don't have rifles or automatic weapons or anything?" Randy asked.

"This isn't a movie," Hank said. "Given that our route on the Amazon crosses the boundaries of multiple countries, it's more trouble than it's worth to have much in the way of firepower aboard. Not only do most of the park services and environmental groups frown on shooting creatures that could be endangered, but once in a while, you'll run across patrol boats trying to prevent weapons smuggling. Anything more threatening than a small revolver gets you the kind of attention from them that you simply don't want."

"Do you at least have more machetes?" Erin asked.

"One," Morgan said. "And since you're the one that asked, and you seem like maybe you can handle yourself, I guess that means you're the one that gets to have it."

"What about me?" Randy asked. "Why can't I have it?"

"Because I'm not an idiot," Morgan said. "Now everybody get to work. This boat isn't going to travel to the mad scientist's secret Amazonian lair all by itself."

12

For the next hour, little of consequence happened, which was good for all of them. All four remaining people on the Lucky Lucy were exhausted, and if they wanted to keep another fight from happening, each of them needed the down time to process the horrible events that had happened so far. Morgan stayed in the cabin, not only keeping control of the wheel but also obsessively checking the sonar to make sure the *Titanoboa* wasn't trying to sneak up behind them. Erin, after Hank had checked her ribs to make sure they were merely bruised rather than broken, had gone below deck to rest.

As much as Hank would have liked to join her, he felt like he needed to be alone at the moment. He'd thought for a while now that this could very well be his last expedition in the field, but now he was all but certain. Field work was never easy, and it certainly didn't get any easier when he was forced to watch the people he was with die in multiple terrible ways, but that wasn't what was really weighing on him at this exact moment. Instead, he couldn't stop thinking about how he'd been forced to stop and take a break during their attempt to journey through the rainforest. He supposed he couldn't completely blame that for what had happened, but he still had to wonder. Would things have been different if he hadn't stopped, if he hadn't ended up splitting the group? Logically, he didn't think it would have changed what happened. If anything, he might have unwittingly helped them. He and Erin had been behind to notice the *Titanoboa* was after them, after all. If they had all been together, maybe the snake's surprise attack would have been more devastating.

Of course, his more emotional side denied all of that. That part of him insisted that he had to have been the cause of Katherine's death, and while he was at it, he might as well accept the blame for Stu and Jasmine. Three people dead, maybe even with more to come, and none of would have happened if some past-his-sell-date professor hadn't still been trying to play Indiana Jones. It was probably just time he admitted that none of this was the right place for him anymore.

"It's not your fault," Randy said to him. Hank started at his voice, then turned to see the young man coming up behind him on the deck. The rain had slowed down to little more than a humid haze hanging over the river, and Hank would have thought that Randy would be somewhere trying to avoid the damp. And while Randy certainly looked miserable as he approached Hank, his foul mood didn't seem to be caused by the weather. In fact, Randy looked like he might have been crying.

"How did you know that was what I was thinking?" Hank asked.

"Because that's what I was thinking, that somehow my lack of experience out here caused Katherine's death," Randy said.

"I thought you blamed the captain."

"I kind of still do. But, well, with three people dead, there's a lot of blame to be spread around."

"You weren't at fault, though, Randy."

"I know. It's in our nature to try to find things to blame in cases like this, even if that blame has to go on yourself. But in this case, maybe the only thing to blame is the giant fricking snake."

Hank nodded, almost ready to concede the point, when he saw something beyond Randy, beyond the boat even, within the floodplain trees. "Uh, or we could blame the giant frog, too. That's a possibility."

"What the hell are you even…?" Randy's voice trailed off as he turned to see what had caught Hank's attention. "Oh wow."

Hank called out so that the others could hear. "Hey, Morgan? Erin? You two better come see this."

As they waited for Erin and the captain to arrive, the two of them stared at the creature clutching the bark of one of the trees. The boat continued on, getting closer to the edge of the tree line where it sat, and with every foot they got closer, Hank expected to find that they had to be seeing some kind of illusion, a trick of the eye that made something tiny actually appear massive. And with every foot, he was proven wrong.

Finally, both Morgan and Erin arrived. All four of them stared at the crazy sight in silence for several moments before Morgan broke their reverie.

"You wanted to find new specimens of frogs, didn't you? Well, there it is."

"That's not helping, Morgan," Hank said.

Normally, tree frogs were supposed to get their names from the fact that they lived up in trees. This one that clung among the low branches might as well have been called that because it was the *size* of a small tree. Its bright green and red coloring suggested that it was probably poisonous, and like the piranhas they had seen earlier, there were variations in its shape from what Hank was used to in tree frogs.

"Is…is a frog that size even supposed to be possible?" Randy asked.

Hank shook his head. "The largest frog currently in existence is supposed to be the goliath frog. And those live in Cameroon, not anywhere in South America."

"What about not currently in existence?" Erin asked. "Could it be some kind of throwback like the *Titanoboa* or those freaky piranhas we saw?"

"The known fossil record for frogs doesn't show anything of that size. And there are certain aspects of their physiology that would suggest that kind of size for them is impossible."

"News flash," Randy said. "It's obviously not."

Hank wanted to ask Morgan to get the *Lucky Lucy* closer to the trees so he could get a better look at the creature, but as much as his scientific curiosity demanded to be sated, he knew there were other things more important at this time. "We don't have time to stop and study it, but we need to at least get a picture or a video. If I go back to the Folger Institute and claim this without some kind of proof, I'd be laughed out of there faster than you could say 'Kermit.'"

"Please tell me this isn't going to be like the last time you tried to get proof of a freaky creature," Randy said. "Or have you forgotten what happened last night when you tried to grab the giant mutant piranha?"

Hank went quiet. Erin had to be the one to say something in response. "Randy, bringing up the death of one our friends just because you don't want to get near a frog? Ultimate dick move."

"We don't even need to get that close," Hank said. He rifled through his gear in his own pack until he came out with a camera phone. He aimed it at the incredible frog sticking to its tree, snapped a few pictures, and then put it away.

As Hank looked away to stash the camera, Randy tugged at his sleeve. "Uh, I think you attracted its attention."

Hank looked up to see that the enormous tree frog was no longer clinging to its tree, but rather had plopped down in the shallow flood waters at the tree's base. It also seemed to be eyeing them all on the deck of the *Lucky Lucy*.

"You know," Randy said, "it suddenly occurs to me that to something that size, we all probably look like a bunch of exotic bugs."

"Maybe," Hank said. "But we shouldn't have anything to worry about. There's still too much distance between us and the edge of the river. I'm sure it can't, uh, it can't…"

The frog was shimmying in their direction, like it was trying to get a good grip on the mud just below the water so it could properly launch itself at them. Hank did some quick calculations in his head. Given the frog's increased size, if its muscles were still proportionate to that of a regular-sized frog, and if he carried the two…

"Everyone, I think we have a problem," Hank said.

This declaration was followed immediately by a giant poisonous tree frog leaping across the expanse of open water to land right on the deck of the *Lucky Lucy*.

Before anyone could panic, Hank held up his hands for calm. "Everyone, just keep cool," he said. "It's, uh, it's probably more scared of us than we are of it."

Randy looked less than convinced. "That doesn't look like the face of something that's scared. That looks like something that is trying to decide what to grab from the buffet."

While the frog didn't look quite large enough to fit any of them in its mouth, it did at least look like it might give it the old college try. The frog croaked at them, a deeper sound than anything Hank had ever heard from an amphibian before. Hank was torn between intense joy and scientific curiosity, and a growing dread that there was no way this particular incident couldn't end badly.

The frog shuffled a little, its bulbous eyes swiveling to take them all in, until its gaze finally settled on the smallest, most bite-sized member of their party.

Erin.

Hank would have screamed for her to watch out, but the frog's tongue was already leaving its mouth and zooming in her direction. While most frogs had tongues that were significantly shorter than pop culture would have people believe, this one's tongue was twice the length of the creature's own body, easily crossing the distance between it and Hank's girlfriend.

Hank closed his eyes. It would happen too fast. The tip of the tongue would hit her, stick to her, and then draw her in, where its mouth would snap shut over her small body. He wouldn't have time to tell her that he wanted more with her, that he only cared about their age difference because that was what society said he should be worried about.

There was a scream of anguish, but it wasn't from Erin. Hank risked opening his eyes. The frog, having now pulled what was left of its tongue back into its mouth, was bleeding profusely as the overly large creature scampered backward in obvious pain and panic. The largest portion of its tongue was lying on the deck, its muscles still twitching as though it thought it was still attached to the frog and just needed to try a little harder to get back in its mouth. Erin stood over the severed tongue with the frog's blood running down the sharp edge of her machete. She looked just as surprised as anyone else that she had chopped off the tongue in time to save herself, but she didn't let that shock slow her down. She reflexively kicked at the offending appendage, knocking the twitching muscle under the lowest rung of the railing and into the water below.

Hank knew immediately what the sudden frenzy of activity in the river meant as the tongue vanished under the surface. The frog was not the only impossible creature with them at the moment. The piranhas were back.

The frog, now in survival mode rather than hunting mode,

gave a short hop in the general direction away from Erin. Unfortunately, that meant it went directly into Randy. Randy, already off balance from all the activity, stumbled backward right into the opposite railing. Hank ran to him, trying to steady him before he went over the railing, but the frog chose that particular moment to jump to what it probably thought was freedom from its attackers. The frog smashed Randy again, pushing him those last vital inches needed to send him toppling into the Amazon.

Morgan, thankfully, was quicker than Hank. He reached out and grabbed Randy by the leg, but he didn't let go of his machete in time to keep the blade from ripping right through the young man's pants leg.

Randy dangled there, his head only a foot or so above the water, as the frog leaped over them to splash into the Amazon. Although it probably would have been able to swim in any other circumstances, the frog hadn't expected the water to suddenly be full of alpha predators. The mutant piranhas instantly swarmed over it, ripping it apart and staining the water with its blood, which only whipped the creatures into a further frenzy. They sensed the blood in the water, and they wanted more.

Unfortunately for Randy, the blood was dripping down his leg, sliding over his chest and face, giving the piranhas another perfect target for their appetites.

"Pull him up!" Hank screamed. "Pull him up before…"

One of the piranhas jumped out of the water, narrowly missing the flesh of Randy's forehead. A second one jumped, this one almost getting tangled in his hair.

"Hurry!" Randy screamed.

Erin joined Hank and Morgan as they struggled to pull Randy back onto the right side of the railing. The piranhas kept jumping, getting more aggressive with each attack and often missing Randy by only the narrowest of margins.

Then Randy was back on their side of the railing, and all of them collapsed in a heavy-breathing heap. The piranhas, apparently recognizing that they weren't going to get their second course here, dispersed for now. Hank had no doubt that they would be back at the slightest sign of vulnerability.

13

"Ow! Son of a bitch!"

"Jesus Christ, Randy," Morgan said as he pulled the bandage tight over Randy's wound. The bleeding had stopped, thankfully, and the gash immediately behind his knee didn't look too deep. The cut on his calf, on the other hand, would have probably required stitches if any of them knew how to do it. Instead, they'd simply had to hope that binding the wound tight enough would suffice until they could get Randy out of here and to proper medical professionals. "I get that it's painful, but show a little perspective. You didn't get eaten by a giant frog."

While the two of them bickered, Hank had taken out his biological sample collection kit and did he best to collect DNA that the frog might have left behind. A few drops of blood, severed pieces of its tongue, and some mucus from its mouth had been left behind before it had taken its final dive into the Amazon, and despite everything else happening, Hank couldn't resist the deep need to get further evidence of the frog's existence. Erin, who had gone to get the second machete while Morgan had been doing his best with Randy's leg, watched Hank fall back into scientist mode with an amused grin on her face.

Morgan pulled the bandage on Randy's leg one final time to make sure it was tight, then backed away to inspect his handiwork. "There. You're not going to bleed to death." He turned to face Erin and Hank. "Are you thinking the same thing that I'm thinking?"

"I'm not sure I know you well enough yet to answer that question," Erin said.

"I might," Hank said. "You're thinking that if we're running into giant impossible frogs, then we have to be getting close to Dr. Sanderton's work site."

"Yeah, pretty much," the captain said.

"How many more miles do we have to go according to the map?" Hank asked.

"Let's go check," Morgan said. He looked over his shoulder at Randy. "And I mean all of us. If there's anything else like that frog out there, it's probably best if we stay locked up inside up until we absolutely can't stay in there anymore."

Once they were all back inside the cabin with the door securely shut, Morgan spent some time going over the sonar data just to make sure that the *Titanoboa* wasn't behind them again. Then he took out the maps they had found on the *Scarman's Chance* and laid them out for everyone to see.

"We're right about here," Morgan said, indicating a specific spot on the river. "And Sanderton's camp, if that's really what we're heading towards, should be right here." He pointed at the island in the middle of the Amazon River. According to the map, it was only about three miles ahead of them now.

"Hell, we should be there in no time, shouldn't we?" Randy asked.

"Usually, yes. But take a look here." He brought all of them over to the ship's instruments. While most of them were completely foreign to Hank, he did clearly recognize the fuel indicator. It was right on the edge of empty.

"We're already slowing down, and there's nothing I can do to speed us back up without fuel," Morgan said. "If we can't find anything on Sanderton's island, then we are well and truly screwed."

"So at our current pace, how long until we get there?" Hank asked.

"Ten minutes, maybe fifteen. We're basically going at the speed of the river now, with any fuel we still have being used purely for fighting against the current when we need to."

"Are we going to take this time to prepare?" Erin asked.

"Sure, not that there's much of anything we can get ready for," Morgan said.

While the two of them discussed what it was even possible for them to do at the moment, Hank's attention wandered to the scene outside the window. He stared for several seconds before he truly registered what he was seeing. "Hey, guys? It looks like we've got more wrecked boats out there."

All of them got closer to the window to see. At the edge of their vision in the hazy atmosphere, they could see the island beginning to loom up out of the mist. There was nothing particularly remarkable about it. There were plenty of islands both large and small littered throughout the Amazon River, and all of them pretty much looked the same. The only difference was that this one had three more boats like the *Scarman's Chance* broken and stranded around its nearest shore. While the nearest one looked more or less intact, the other two had clearly come to grief from something large and angry. Hank didn't even have to guess at what that something might have been.

"Are all of these like the *Scarman's Chance?*" Randy asked. "I mean, were they supply boats for this Sanderton woman?"

Morgan shrugged. "I couldn't tell you."

"Have there been any other recent reports of missing boats in the area?" Hank asked.

"Not that I've heard, but like I said earlier, I wasn't even positive that the *Scarman's Chance* had vanished. The Amazon River is very long, and there's any number of spots between the wild places that boats could stop to rest or restock."

He said he didn't want to get any closer to the other boats to check their names, either. According to Morgan, he simply didn't want to waste any of their precious gas checking on boats that they all knew were beyond rescue. Hank suspected, however, that what he really didn't want was to approach them and find the remains of one of his captain friends.

Randy, however, didn't seem to be aware that approaching the wrecked boats might be a sensitive subject. "Can't we just search all of those boats for fuel?" While Morgan bristled, Hank answered for him.

"We need to at least check the island, one way or the other. If we don't find what we need there, we can always use the other boats as a possible backup plan."

"Uh, and what if I don't want to stop on the mysterious mist-shrouded island of the evil super genius?" Randy asked.

"I told you before. She's not evil," Hank said.

"Hank, just relax," Erin said, then smiled. "If I didn't know any better, I'd say you're so desperate to believe that she can't be behind this because you've slept with her at some point in the past."

Hank blushed. "I have not. Well, okay, maybe I did have a crush on her for all of five minutes, but let's be honest. Most of us scientists don't get laid very much. It's easy to distract us with someone of our preferred gender. But that's not the reason at all. I respect her. I always have, even when some people had problems with her ideas or methods. If she really is responsible for all the aberrations we've been saying, then it has to be because something is wrong with her."

The closer they got to the island, the more ominous it seemed to get, if that was even possible after the boat graveyard they had already seen. Maybe it was just a trick of his imagination, but to Hank, the trees on the island seemed darker, and the natural noises of the wild seemed more muted as they approached.

Erin was apparently thinking the same thing. "I don't hear as many birds or animals," she said. "That's never a good sign."

"Come on, everyone," Morgan said. "Time to start leaving the safety of the cabin and start the prep for landing."

"Where are we even going to anchor the boat?" Hank asked. "We can't anchor it too far from the shore this time and use the rowboats. We already know for a fact that those piranhas are still nearby, and while the *Lucky Lucy* has proven resilient to them so far, I doubt the rowboats will be as sturdy."

The captain shook his head. "We shouldn't have to worry about that. The map showed that there were docks enough for four or five boats. We should find them just around the south side of the island."

They hadn't gone far along toward the docks when Erin pointed something out in the shallow flood waters. "Hey, guys? Take a look at that. Is that what I think it is?"

Hank and the others joined her at the railing. "If you think that's a human skeleton," Morgan said softly, "then yeah, I think it is."

It didn't take a genius to figure out what exactly had happened to the poor schmuck half-sticking out of the mud. They didn't even need to get that close to see the very clear teeth marks from the piranhas all over the white bones. There wasn't any sign of who the person might have been, but the bones were completely picked clean and didn't look like they had been sitting there for too long.

"Okay, seriously," Randy said. "If ever I saw a sign that said 'don't fricking step foot on this island,' that's it right there."

"For the last time, we don't have a choice, Randy," Hank

said. "If we're going to get any answers at all as to why three of our people are dead and there are things roaming the Amazon that have no right to be there, then we have to get off here."

"Yeah, and when we do, we'll probably never be setting foot on this boat again," Randy muttered under his breath.

Whoever had written on the maps that there would be multiple docks had lied. They couldn't even say for certain if there was even one dock. The broken wooden structure they came to looked like it had been a dock once, and probably within the relatively recent past. Several pieces of flotsam floating in the nearby water suggested there had been small motor or rowboats tied up here, but they had been smashed to pieces just like the dock. There was at least enough of the dock left that they could tie the boat to it, but that was all.

"That's roughly where the maps said the landing for the island would be," Erin said. "So this has to be the place."

"I'm still not thinking this is a good idea," Randy said.

"So you've said repeatedly," Hank said. "And we've been ignoring. Please buy a clue, already."

"I'm just saying, this reminds me too much of that book where someone goes down the river and finds a crazy guy living deep in the jungle."

"*Heart of Darkness*," Erin said. "And yeah, there certainly are a few eerie similarities."

"If nothing else, we should stop here to rest," Morgan said. "But best case scenario, if this Dr. Sanderton really is here and things aren't as dire as we're afraid of, she might have some communications equipment we can use to call for help, or even extra fuel."

"Or she might try to feed us to the mutant prehistoric creatures she's breeding," Randy said.

As much as Hank wanted to again deny that Dr. Sanderton had anything to do with the strange creatures they'd been seeing, he couldn't ignore any longer that the world's foremost paleo-geneticist just so happened to have a mysterious camp right around the same area where a prehistoric snake had suddenly appeared. Logic dictated that she must have something to do with it all, or at the very least be studying whatever was happening here. "We don't really have any choice but to stop and look for her," Hank said.

"True enough," Morgan said with a sigh. "Come on. Let's do our best to tie up the *Lucky Lucy* to that pile of rotted sticks over there. We've got a possibly prion-infected scientist to visit."

"Sounds oh so very fun," Randy muttered, but he did as he was told.

14

Wait. I think I remember something.

It was a thought she had often these days, even if it turned out that she wasn't remembering anything of value at all. But this, she thought, had something to do with the *Titanoboa* sample she'd used to create her first specimen. Running into the tent that acted more or less as her office, she found it in disarray. Had someone been in her recently to ransack it? She thought so at first, then remembered that this was simply the way it always was. There was a table in the center piled high with refuse, and a rusty stool next to it. She had a cot at the far end, but she never used it anymore. Most of the time, she just slept on the ground.

Sanderton cleared away the discarded potato chip bags that had been taking over the table so that she could properly spread out her maps for the first time in months. Given the information she had gotten out of her last supplier, she thought she might finally be able to find the right fossils she needed. She put a finger on the map, slowly tracing a path from her current location to the coordinates she'd been given, then added in a few of her own calculations. Right there. So close to where her camp currently was that it had practically been under her nose this entire time. She put her palms to her temples, trying to concentrate. Yes, that's right, she was supposed to know that was there all along, wasn't she?

Ignoring the voice in her head trying to tell her that something was seriously wrong with her, Sanderton ran out of the shed and made a beeline for the area beyond her camp where the sample was supposed to be. There was a stone outcropping here that had obviously been chipped away at recently, and in it were several impressions that looked like small snake skeletons in eggs. The preservation of the soft tissues in the fossil was astonishing, beyond anything Sanderton had ever seen before. Except, she had seen them before, right? The marks in the fossil even suggested that she had taken samples from here in the past.

Annalisa, wake up! the voice in her head screamed. *Your brain is Swiss-cheesed.* Just as quickly as that voice had appeared in her head, it had already vanished deep into her increasingly unstable memory. All that stayed with her was that there must be genetic material here, given how unusually well-preserved it was, that could help her properly prepare the new *Titanoboa* egg that she'd been struggling with only yesterday.

Sanderton took a scraping from the same part of the fossil that she had last time (not that she actually remembered doing so), then ran back into Camp Anthropocene and directly to the shed where she kept the incubators. It took quite some time to prepare the genetic material she'd found in the sample, but the customized CRISPR samples and machines she had among her technological arsenal were able to make quick work of the damaged DNA, giving her something proper to inject the egg with. Using the shell of an anaconda egg (or maybe she should switch to an ostrich egg? Wait, had she already had this conversation with herself?), she started the process again, and was just finishing up when the lights on her work table started lighting up with the silent proximity alarm. The alarm actually went off on a fairly regular basis, considering how many animals freely roamed her cozy little island in the middle of the Amazon River. Yet every single time, even though it almost always seemed to be some large cat or capybara or something, she was dead convinced the alarm meant some spy was here to sabotage her work.

She went over to a bank of small monitors nearby linked to various security cameras she had placed around the camp. Most of them showed nothing but static or a blank screen. The cameras had been failing one by one, and despite her paranoia, she kept forgetting to try fixing them. At least one was still working over by the docks, though, giving her a rather interesting show. She leaned closer, staring at the boat that had pulled up to dock at the entrance of her little island hideaway. She had visitors. Given that she'd released certain throwback versions of piranhas just to ensure that anyone who had previously been her supplier never left the Amazon, she knew that these people couldn't possibly be with the *Scarman's Chance,* or any of the other boats that had come and gone from here with no chance of ever making it back to civilization. That meant that the only possible reason these people could be here was if they were spies trying to steal her research.

No, Annalisa, that doesn't make any…

The warning voice in her head faded away. It was getting harder and harder to hear it recently. Maybe that meant the voice was a sign of madness and she was finally getting better.

"Yay, I'm getting better," she whispered to herself, then added. "Getting better from what?" She shook her head, trying to rid herself of the intrusive thoughts and stay focused on the task at hand. On the camera, the people on the boat found the least trashed of the docks, the only one that still even looked like a dock instead of just broken tree trunks in the water, and began tying off to it.

"Yes, yes," she muttered to herself. "I've been looking forward to this part." Just like so much of what she said to herself these days, she wasn't entirely sure if that were true, but it was a suitably villain-like phrase, so she went with it. She left the monitors and went over to a locked metal cabinet in the corner of the shed. They key was already in the lock. She never took it out now. She'd lost it too many times. She wanted to keep the items inside safe from people that might invade her camp, but she also didn't want to have to go searching for the key when she needed it most, so this felt like the most logical compromise.

She opened the door and took out the item inside. Among the last shipment she had received from one of the supply boats before she'd had the boat "taken care of" had been this particular beauty. Sanderton had never been particularly fond of guns, but at around the same time she had realized she was truly supposed to be among the "evil mastermind" persuasion, she had realized she couldn't be a true villain without weaponry. And so she had purchased this bad boy, a Soviet Union-era Kalashnikov, specifically the infamous AK-47. She checked the magazine to make sure it was full, then locked the cabinet back up.

She wished she had a full-length mirror to look at herself in, but the only thing she had in the camp was a broken hand mirror. Oh well. She knew exactly how much she looked like an evil badass, and that was all that mattered.

Well, that, and also that she scared the crap out of her visitors before she killed them. She had to keep her priorities straight, after all.

She ran out of the shed, her rifle held loosely in her hand, so that she could prepare a proper place for her visitors before they arrived at camp.

15

There wasn't a lot of the dock left for them to tie the boat to, so that actually had to tie it up in several places. Getting off the *Lucky Lucy* was an equally perilous adventure, given that the broken pier often threatened to give out under foot and send them plunging into the Amazon. While there was no immediate sign of piranhas in the water, either super or regular, none of them were keen to test that out.

The rain and mist had started to lift, though, giving them a better view of the island that would either be their last chance at safety or else would put them face to face with a madwoman. The rotting dock went over the flooded areas all the way onto the muddy but otherwise dry land, and the four of them carefully made their way over the spongy boards until they were sure that the ground beneath them wouldn't suddenly give way. Both Morgan and Erin had their machetes, but it didn't look like they would need them to get deeper into the island. There was a well-worn path here, which Hank could only assume led directly to Sanderton's camp.

Even with the clear path, though, the going was slow. Randy's leg was still very much a problem, and all kept close to him. They were, after all, still remembering what had happened the last time they'd tried to go over land and someone among them had fallen behind. They didn't want a repeat.

After a couple minutes of walking, Morgan stopped them. "Hold on. Just listen for a second."

They all did as he said. The sound that had caught his attention was immediately noticeable. Somewhere behind them, something wooden snapped with a loud crack. Everyone knew exactly what might be behind them that was powerful enough to snap something. Whether it was a tree, the boat, or part of the docks didn't matter. The *Titanoboa* was behind them somewhere, and something was getting crushed under its massive weight. If they stayed around here, they would be next.

Morgan, Erin, and Hank started to run, but Hank called for the other two to halt when he realized that Randy wasn't joining them. Instead, he stood right in the middle of the path facing the direction of the giant monster that would be pursuing them any second now.

"Randy, you dumbass, what are you doing?" Morgan asked.

"This is it for me," Randy said. "My leg is too messed up. I'd only slow you down. The rest of you go on ahead. I'll do what I can to, uh, distract it. You need to be as far away as possible by the time it's finished with me."

"No," Morgan said.

"No? What do you mean no? You aren't honestly going to try to get me to come with you, are you? You don't even like me."

"Randy, just because you're an asshole doesn't mean I'm going to let you end up in a snake's stomach. Now quit acting like you think you're a hero and get moving, before I bash you over the head with a branch and drag you out of that thing's reach by your hair."

Randy paused as though he actually had to consider it, or

maybe he was just surprised that Morgan was actually acting semi-protective of him. Either way, Randy turned to run with them, or at least as close to a run as he could manage with the gash on his leg bleeding again. The four of them moved as quickly as they could through the underbrush, but Hank couldn't help but remember how fast the *Titanoboa* had been when chasing them over the ground earlier. Given the fact that it had just recently eaten Katherine, a snake like that shouldn't have been hungry again so soon, but Hank wasn't going to take any chances.

"Wait. Did you hear that?" Erin asked. "It sounded like something hissing."

The rest of them didn't need to pause and listen. The hiss was loud enough that they could even hear it through the rustle of leaves and brush something humongous moved through the forest towards them.

"Move!" Morgan yelled.

The underbrush here wasn't nearly as thick as when they had first tried to go overland, likely due to the fact that someone else had been walking through this area frequently. It made their going easier as they ran, but Hank still thought he could hear the gigantic monster following them catching up. Randy almost fell behind several times, but Erin, despite still nursing her damaged ribs from earlier in the day, grabbed him by the arm and pulled him along. The farther they ran, the more signs they found that they must be approaching some kind of camp, and not a very well maintained one, either. If Hank hadn't suspected that his life might have been on the line if he dared slow down and contemplate what he saw, he would have been appalled by the crushed Mountain Dew cans and discarded Hostess wrappers that littered the ground. Most scientists in the field would have done everything in their power to avoid contaminating a site like this. To Hank, that only seemed to further prove that something had seriously gone wrong with the formerly respected Dr. Sanderton. That impression was reinforced as they ran past a sign declaring the place to Camp Anthropocene, painted on a slab of wood in the sort of shaky, uneven letters of a child.

As they got closer and Hank could start to make out tents and structures hidden among the vines, he noticed several poles set up around the camp at regular intervals. Each of the poles seemed to be wired to a small generator, and Hank could hear and feel the distinct hum of electricity coming from each of them. He'd seen something like them used at a few research sites in the past where there was concern of wild animal attacks, so he had a pretty good idea of what they were and why they were there.

"That's a sonic fence!" Hank said to the others. "Quick, we all have to get to the other side before –"

From behind them somewhere, it sounded like something had knocked over a small tree. Everyone rushed to the area beyond the poles, but while the others seemed inclined to continue running, Hank stopped and turned around.

"Hank, what the hell are you doing?" Erin said to him. "The snake is still –"

"Just wait for it," Hank said. For the first time since this expedition had begun, he allowed himself a smug and knowing smile.

The *Titanoboa* came through the trees behind them, a prehistoric monster out of humanity's most primal nightmares. It slithered directly toward them at an impossible speed, and Hank almost caught himself flinching. When it was within fifteen feet of the fence, however, the snake slowed to a stop. For several seconds, it looked confused, or possibly even in pain. Then it slowly turned around and started heading in the opposite direction.

Morgan and Erin came back to Hank's side to join him, while Randy leaned against a tree in order to keep from falling over. "What the hell was that about?" Morgan asked.

Hank pointed at the nearest pole. "The sonic fence. It's like a variation on some of the technology you sometimes see used to keep dogs from wandering out of their yard. The pole emits a high-pitched frequency that most humans can't hear, but most animals can. Sanderton must be using it to keep the bigger wild creatures at bay."

"Good," Morgan said. He turned back around to look at the sorry state of the camp. "This can't really be it, can it?"

"What exactly were you expecting?" Hank asked.

"This woman is probably infected with some maddening brain disease and recreating giant prehistoric monsters that kill anyone that gets too close to her secret island base," Morgan said. "I was at least expecting, oh, I don't know, a bunker of some kind? Sentry gun turrets. Instead, we get some ratty tents, a few sheds from IKEA, and a junk food habit." He kicked at a Ho-Ho wrapper on the ground. "This place doesn't exactly support the idea that she's behind all this."

"Oh, but I am," a voice said from one of the nearby sheds.

When last he had seen Dr. Annalisa Sanderton, Hank had thought she looked about as stereotypically like a nerdy scientist as possible. Now all that nerdiness was gone, and in its place was a woman that looked like she had gone completely feral. Her hair was a tangled bird's nest, complete with what might have been actual bird shit along with all the other mud and grime. The dirt on her face obscured most of her features, and it was only the shape of her nose and chin that confirmed to Hank that this was indeed the woman he had previously met at various conferences. She somehow managed to look both malnourished and chubby at the same time, thanks to her stick-like appendages yet slightly distended gut. The biggest and most important difference, however, was in her eyes. Long gone were the intensity and quiet kindness he had once thought he'd seen in them. Instead, they looked wild, the eyes of someone who probably believed every conspiracy theory she was told before even making up a few of her own.

And to make matters worse, she was holding an AK-47 against her hip. Although she didn't seem to have the slightest clue about how to properly hold it, she did have it aimed directly at them all.

"Welcome to my evil lair," she said. "I'm Doctor Annalisa Sanderton, and I'll be your evil genius mad scientist for this evening. You all, on the other hand, are going to be my captives."

16

They all instinctively raised their hands in surrender. Both Morgan and Erin dropped their machetes to the ground, although Dr. Sanderton barely even seemed to register that they had been armed.

"Dr. Sanderton, please hold on for just a second," Hank said. "I'm sure there's been some kind of misunderstanding."

"Hank, just accept it already," Morgan said to him. "Her train no longer goes all the way to the station."

Hank ignored him. "My compatriots here think something sinister might be going on, but I told them that I know you. There must be some kind of explanation for all this."

Sanderton cocked her head and blinked several times. "We know each other? I don't think that's right. I think I would remember meeting someone as old as you."

Hank paused, unsure for a moment how to address that, before continuing on as though he hadn't noticed the insult. "It's me, Dr. Hank Newstead. Remember? We've met at a couple of scientific conferences. We don't know each other especially well, but we talked at length."

For a few breaths, she appeared to believe him before

something dark passed over her face. "No. I've never met you. You can't fool me. You're just here to steal my research and stop my diabolical plan."

Now it was Hank's turn to be confused. "Diabolical plan?"

She walked closer to them, waving her gun at all of them erratically. Hank could see Morgan considering trying to grab it from her, but Hank stopped him with a minute shake of his head. His worst fears for Dr. Sanderton were being confirmed here. She was obviously highly unstable, and there was no telling what unhinged thing she might do if Morgan tried to defy her.

"Of course, diabolical plan. If you claim to know me, then you should have heard by now. I'm a super villain. It's actually really cool."

She walked around the group to inspect them. When she was right behind Randy, he tried to say something. "Super villain? Are you serious? This isn't a comic book or a James Bond..."

Sanderton kicked Randy in the back of his bad knee, forcing him to drop to the ground with a squeal of pain. "That was surprisingly fun," she said. "Actually, all of this is kind of fun. I should have tried being the bad guy earlier in life."

"Dr. Sanderton, what happened to you?" Hank asked.

"What happened? Nothing happened. I'm perfectly..." Her words trailed off as she stared into space for several seconds.

"Sanderton, listen to me," Hank said. "Based on everything I've seen, I think you might have been infected with one of the prions you were studying when you were in Eastern Europe."

"I was never studying prions," Sanderton said, then again looked lost, like her mind couldn't stay in one place for too long. "Was I?"

"This isn't really you," Hank said. "You're sick. Let all this go so that we can help you."

"No," Sanderton said as she shook her head. "No, I can't. I'm doing too much good here."

"It's no use, Hank," Morgan said. "She's too far gone. Whatever those prion-things have done to her brain, there's not going to be any talking sense to her."

"Please, just let us go," Erin pleaded to her.

"That's not something evil masterminds do, is it?" Sanderton asked. Coming from anyone else, that would have been a rhetorical question, but she said it as though it were an actual question she was unsure about and wanted the others to answer. When no one answered her, she frowned and shook her head. "No, I don't think it is." She waved the Kalashnikov at all of them. "Okay, kiddies, come on. I've got a cage just big enough to fit all of you in it."

Hank looked around at the others to see if anyone was going to be foolhardy enough to challenge the woman with a Soviet-era automatic rifle. Erin held up her hands passively, while Morgan stayed on guard but willing to obey. Randy was the only one who looked like he might be trouble, although not because he wanted to disobey their new captor. Sanderton's kick had reopened the wounds on his calf and knee. His bandages were darkening with blood again, and although he couldn't have lost that much blood so far, he looked ready to faint from the exertion. Hank grabbed him by an armpit before he could collapse and once again bring on Sanderton's strange wrath.

Sanderton herded them among the pre-fab sheds to the largest structure in the camp. Keeping her rifle aimed squarely at them, she punched in the numbers on a security keypad at the door. When the keypad buzzed and flashed red, she did it again. Then again. Only after five tries did she get the security code right, yet she didn't act like this was a problem. In fact, five seconds after she opened the door, she didn't even seem to remember that the code had been giving her trouble. Hank would have dwelled on that fact, but the sight beyond the door caught all his attention and took his breath away.

"Oh my God," he whispered. Sanderton looked over at him with unrestrained pride, her joy obvious at having someone else around that could appreciate what she had done. The room was full of shelves, all of them packed tight with cages and aquariums. Nothing currently in the shed was quite at the size of the creatures they had already seen on the river, but Hank knew enough to realize that most of these things weren't supposed to exist anymore.

"You like it?" Sanderton asked. Hank couldn't help but nod in morbid appreciation. He moved closer to the nearest set of aquariums. Erin touched his arm, likely expecting his movement to send Sanderton into a sudden fit, but the scientist let him have his look. This particular cage was filled with his specialty: frogs. And unless he was mistaken, most of these frogs shouldn't have been able to live in the wild anymore. A Rabb's fringe-limbed tree frog sat at the front of the aquarium staring at Hank with huge, almost adorable eyes. The last survivor of the species was supposed to have died off in September of 2016, and yet here one was. No, wait, not one. Two. Sanderton actually had a mating pair here, and from the looks of the shallow water in the aquarium with them, they had succeeded in their job and produced eggs.

"How are you even keeping them alive?" Hank asked, indicating the two frogs. "This tank is hardly sealed against all the elements. Shouldn't the chytrid fungus be getting in and killing them?"

"Ooh, now you're speaking my language," Sanderton said. "I have to periodically inject them with a serum that will keep them alive. It's really temperamental, too; if I don't get the formula exactly right, it wouldn't just kill them but any amphibian and reptile. I keep the serum…" She paused, then smiled. "Ah, you almost had me. Sorry, but I'm not going to sit and explain all the science to someone that's obviously here to steal all my trade secrets."

Hank didn't bother to correct her, as he was soon once again distracted by the tanks and cages. Although the Rabb's frogs had naturally been the first ones he'd noticed, they weren't anywhere near as impressive as some of the other specimens Sanderton had in her care. There were multiple tanks with fist-sized bugs in them, along with added air tanks on the side to provide the over-sized insects with the additional oxygen larger bugs would need. One particularly large aquarium had what might very well have been a trilobite, and a cage hanging near one of the corners seemed to hold an archaeopteryx, a prehistoric bird that was commonly thought to be part of the evolutionary bridge between modern birds and dinosaurs. Hank stared slack-jawed at it. The *Titanoboa* had been impressive, true, but in terms of basic shape, it was still a snake, just a particularly large specimen. But this was a creature that had no real modern equivalent.

What Dr. Sanderton had accomplished here was both brilliant and insane. Science should not have been at this level yet, except here they were. With whatever technology she'd used, it was entirely possible that actual dinosaurs could be brought back at some point in the future.

He thought of a *Tyrannosaurus* rampaging through downtown New York, then shuddered.

At the very back of the shed, there was a cage larger than any of the others. Given its size and the fact that it was empty, Hank could only assume that it had at some point been the home of the *Titanoboa*. Sanderton must have let it out once it became too big to be held here anymore. Now all that remained in it were large discarded snake skins and a number of rather rancid snake turds.

"You want us to get in there?" Randy asked. "I'm pretty sure the Geneva Convention has some pretty strict things to say about that kind of torture."

"Randy, seriously, if you don't knock it off, I'm going to

smack you," Erin said.

"Er, sorry. I use humor when I get upset and nervous."

"No, you *try* to use humor," Erin said. "That doesn't mean you actually succeed."

Sanderton ushered to four of them into the cell, then closed the door behind them and turned the key. As she backed away from the cage, Hank came forward and gripped the bars. "Annalisa, what are you even planning on doing with us?"

"You know? I don't think I know the answer to that yet," Sanderton said. "Actually, wait! I think I do know. I'll keep you around until the second is big enough, then I'll feed you all to it so it can grow big and strong and go join its mate."

Hank felt the hairs raise at the back of his neck. "The second? The second what?"

"The second *Titanoboa*," she answered in a tone that said she couldn't possibly respect anyone who couldn't figure this out for themselves. "I'm pretty sure my work on the egg earlier has been successful this time."

"What are you talking about?" Hank asked.

Sanderton seemed to be so excited to talk about her work that she forgot her paranoia that they were here to steal her secrets, or else she simply thought it didn't matter what they knew now that they were her prisoners. "It's taken me forever, but I finally got a viable sample of *Titanoboa* DNA to implant in another egg. Once it's been incubated long enough, it will hatch, and then there will hopefully be both a male and a female. Once I release the second one into the wild to join the first, then maybe their population can become self-sustaining. And even if that's not enough, I can still make more."

Hank looked at the others to make sure they shared his same look of horror. When he looked back at Sanderton, she was already on her way out the door.

"You four go ahead and get cozy in there," she said. "I'm off to take a nap. See you when I come back to feed you."

She closed the door behind her, leaving them alone to their fate.

Erin leaned against the wall. While everyone else in the cage had despondent expressions on their faces, hers was strangely amused. "Ten bucks says that when she feeds us, it's just some crap like Twinkies or Zingers."

"If she even remembers to feed us at all," Morgan said. "And given her state of mine, I'd even put money on that one."

"We are so screwed," Randy said. "There's no way we can get out of this now. We might as well start making peace with our maker."

"You go ahead and do that," Erin said. "While you're busy with that, if the rest of you don't mind, I'm going to use that precious time to escape instead."

Morgan raised a bemused eyebrow at her. "And how exactly do you propose doing that? Do you happen to have a magical extra key in your back pocket."

Erin started laughing her ass off.

"Uh, Erin?" Hank asked. "I'm glad we could amuse you, but would you mind letting the rest of us in on your joke?"

"Seriously, no one else noticed?" Erin said. "It was right there in front of the faces of the professor, the rugged captain, and the wannabe business major, yet I'm the only one who saw it?"

"Erin, please," Morgan said. "Out with it already."

"Either the good doctor's brain is truly fried by this point, or else she is an epically terrible evil genius." Erin reached through the bars to the lock on the outer side of the cage.

She turned the key, which was still in the lock where Sanderton had left it.

"So are the rest of you coming with me?" Erin asked. "Or were you just planning on staying in here with the snake shit?"

17

Hank waited for Erin to open the door of their cage and then followed her right out into the open. He moved cautiously, sure that this had to be some kind of trap. Dr. Sanderton couldn't possibly be so far gone now that she would have honestly forgotten to take her key out of the lock, right? But as they all filed out of the cage and into the larger portion of the specimen shed, nothing or no one popped out at them to stop them from escaping. Apparently, this was really happening.

"Uh, so what exactly are we going to do now?" Randy asked.

"What the hell do you think we're going to do?" Morgan asked. "We're going to escape."

"We don't even have anywhere to go," Hank said. "The *Lucky Lucy* is completely out of fuel, isn't it?"

"Not completely," Morgan said. "We have just enough to get away from the island."

"And what the hell are we supposed to do from there?" Randy asked.

"Does it matter? For now, it should be enough that we can get away from this place alive. I certainly don't think we're going to be around long if the crazy woman with an automatic rifle has her way."

"That's a fair enough point," Randy said.

"But we can't just run," Erin said. "You heard what she's doing here. The *Titanoboa* is just the tip of the iceberg. If she succeeds in creating a second one..."

Hank finished her thought. "Then there might be a breeding pair. And a breeding pair means that a monster snake species that can swallow humans in an instant and still have room to spare would be unleashed on the planet. We can't let that happen."

"And how the hell exactly are we going to prevent that?" Erin asked. "Do we even know where to begin?"

"I might," Hank said. "She said something when I was asking her about the Rabb's frogs, something about the fungus that has been killing so many amphibians. I might be able to use that to my advantage, if I can find the area of the camp where she's doing the actual breeding and experimenting."

"That shouldn't be too hard," Morgan said. "There's not a lot of places in the camp for us to check."

"Yeah, and not a lot of places where she might be," Randy said. "If we just up and walk out that door, and she happens to be anywhere where she might see us, there would be nothing stopping her from locking us away again, and this time, she might not forget to take the key."

"Maybe, but maybe not," Hank said. "She said something about taking a nap. Her brain may be mush now compared to what it once was, but it used to be that she rarely slept in bed, instead choosing to sleep on the floor, and once she was down, she was legendary for her ability to sleep through anything. It made her the subject of a number of good-natured pranks among colleagues. Hopefully, she's still the same way. We just need to avoid any of the tents that look like she might be using them as her living space."

"Okay then," Morgan said. "You and Randy go to sabotage

her research and make sure nothing like the *Titanoboa* ever comes out of this camp again. Erin and I will go to get our machetes, and I think I may also have an idea that can help us."

Morgan left the shed before Hank could question him further.

Outside the shed, Hank paused long enough to look around and see if perhaps Dr. Sanderton was still around, and that her tale about taking a nap had just been a way to lull them into a false sense of security. The coast was clear, though, except for the fact that he had to be extra careful treading through the soda and Red Bull cans accumulated at the door. This was another clear sign that something had gone terribly wrong in Sanderton's brain. He remembered her refusing to drink anything but water, and she sure as hell would have never left recyclable materials just lying around in the middle of an endangered wilderness. He supposed that one way or the other, this whole thing was the end for her. If she died from her brain disease or if she survived long enough to face the consequences of everything she had done here, a bright mind and a bright career were going to be gone.

They found Sanderton's "lab," such as it was, in the second shed they checked. The first was full of garbage. This explained, at least to some degree, why the rest of the camp was filthy with wrappers and food containers. Apparently, she had started using this shed as her garbage storage, then ran out of the room. The smell inside the hot shed was the unique sort of wretched that Hank had never expected to experience in his entire life, and given the number of very large flies buzzing around inside, not only had the garbage pile been there for a while, but it included a large amount of dead animal and plant matter. Given that Hank hadn't seen anything resembling a toilet around the camp yet, he also suspected the shed might contain more than its share of human excrement.

The second shed was a leap beyond the first, but it still wasn't anywhere near the standards of what any other scientist would have considered a proper laboratory. It was a wonder Sanderton had been able to accomplish anything at all, given all the contamination from the various bits of food and filth she had littered around her workstations.

One station was cleaner than the rest, however, and Hank immediately gravitated toward it. On the table there was an incubator with a single egg inside and a needle off to the side that she must have used to inject it with the proper DNA sample. Despite himself, Hank allowed himself a moment of pure wonder at what she had accomplished. Then he reminded himself what kind of havoc would be caused if this egg ever managed to hatch, and he came back down to Earth.

"So that's it?" Randy asked. "All this fuss over one over-sized egg?"

"That one egg, if allowed to go all the way, will become another *Titanoboa*, in case you forgot."

"No, I didn't forget. It's just kind of amazing, is all. That enormous fricking snake came from something this size, and another one can make it all so much worse."

"Which is exactly why we need to get rid of it," Hank said.

"That should be pretty easy, right?" Randy asked. "All we need to do is take it out and smash it."

Hank shook his head. "That wouldn't be enough. The DNA would still be intact, and Sanderton would just have to prepare it and inject it into another egg. No, we have to do something to irreconcilably taint the sample."

"Then I hope you have some idea how to do that," Randy said. "Because I wouldn't have the first clue."

"I do," Hank said. "Given what she said earlier, some of her specialized chytrid fungus samples should be around here. All I need to do is mess with them to create something that would interfere with the egg, then inject it."

Finding it proved to be the easy part. Sanderton kept it in a nearby test tube marked "Silly Fungus." Altering it took a little more work, but if what she had said earlier was true, he didn't have to be precise.

"Are you sure you have the mixture right?"

"Don't be an idiot, Randy," Hank said. "Of course I don't. That's the whole point. Just a tiny bit wrong, and everything in her experiment gets screwed up."

As he injected the toxic mixture into the egg, however, he had to wonder if he was about to cause more harm than good. The fungus had already caused irreparable harm to the frog population of the Amazon, and here he was creating a supped-up version of it. If this particular version of the fungus spread beyond just the things Sanderton had been breeding here, then the result would be an environmental catastrophe beyond anything the original chytrid fungus had done by itself. Of course, it would have been an even greater disaster if a second *Titanoboa* was suddenly out there, one capable of possibly mating with the first.

"Wait, is that it?" Randy asked as Hank put down the syringe. "I was expecting, I don't know, explosions or something."

It was a shame that Morgan wasn't with them, Hank thought, because he would have very likely called Randy out for being an idiot. As it was, Hank had already called him that once within the last minute, and he didn't want to repeat himself. "Come on," Hank said. "We have to meet Morgan and Erin at the rendezvous point."

As they ran out of the shed, Hank had to force himself not to stop at the shed full of cages again. Sanderton's work here might have been unethical and dangerous, but it was also brilliant. She had done things in paleontology and genetics that had previously not been possible outside science fiction.

"I know that look," Randy said as he grabbed Hank's arm and pulled him away from the shed. "Don't."

"Don't what?"

"Don't stop to try collecting samples to prove what we've seen. Four words, Hank: *mutant piranha* and *giant frog*. You know what happened before. Please don't make this strike number three."

With a begrudging grumble, Hank agreed and followed Randy in the general direction of the broken docks. Just outside the posts for the sonic fence, right near the childish sign announcing the camp's name, they found Erin and the captain waiting for them.

"Where did you two go?" Hank asked them.

"It was the captain's idea," Erin said. She pointed at the nearest visible pole that made up the sonic fence. Hank hadn't noticed it earlier, but now that he was paying attention, he realized they no longer emitted the subtle electric hum that they had earlier. "By disabling the sonic fence, Camp Anthropocene will no longer have quite as much defense against the wild, which means…"

"Which means more outside sources can get in and wreck the camp, including Sanderton's research," Hank said with a nod. Again he felt a pang of regret, but it was the best option for them at the moment.

"Where is Sanderton, anyway?" Randy asked. "Anyone else think it's suspicious that we were able to escape her cage and sabotage both her camp and her experiments without her showing up to stop us?"

"Who the hell even knows with her?" Morgan asked. "It's pretty obvious at this point that the brain-eating prion theory about her is true. She could be running around trying to undo the damage we've done, or she could be talking to herself with sock puppets."

"I don't have any socks," a voice said from somewhere above them. Hank looked up just in time to see Sanderton perched in the branches of a tree, her AK-47 in hand and aimed directly at them. And she didn't look like she was about to give them a chance to stand down.

18

Thankfully, whatever disease was ravaging Sanderton's brain, it also apparently affected her reflexes and motor skills. She was slowing enough at aiming the rifle and pulling the trigger that Hank was able to shove Erin out of her way, while Morgan did the same with Randy. The bullets raked the ground where they had been, kicking up dirt and garbage. Hank pulled Erin under a thick copse of vines on one side of the path while Morgan did the same on the other side. Hank wasn't sure if the foliage completely hid them from Sanderton's view, but the mad scientist continued to fire in the middle of the path as though she thought they would simply come back out and walk right into her line of fire.

"Come out, come out, wherever you are!" she screamed from up in her branch. "Olly olly oxen free!"

From his vantage point, Hank could see the way Captain Morgan was looking at the tree Sanderton had taken refuge in. He knew that look. That was the look of the captain contemplating something brave yet fool-hardy.

The firing stopped. "Oh fine, just go ahead and leave," she said. "See if I care. It's not like I wanted you around anyway."

When none of them moved, she added. "Not falling for it, huh? I just want you to know something. Even if you do escape, it's not going to make any difference. If you tell the rest of the world what I'm doing here, I may have to abandon Camp Anthropocene, but I can just start it again elsewhere."

Given the current state of Sanderton's mental and physical health, Hank very much doubted she would get very far in that, but if she continued at all, she could still wreak havoc. Morgan must have been thinking the same thing, since he scrambled through the bushes to get to the base of Sanderton's tree and immediately started climbing. From her current position, it didn't look like Sanderton could see any of this.

Hank moved closer to Erin. "Looks like it's up to us to keep her distracted," he whispered. She nodded.

"And how exactly do we intend to do that?" she asked.

The answer came to him pretty quickly. "The same way I almost distracted her earlier when she brought us in to our cage. The same way to distract any nerdy type. Express interest in the things they're into."

Hank cleared his throat and then raised his voice loud enough for Sanderton to hear. "Hey, there's something I've been wondering."

"If you're expecting me to tell you my trade secrets, you can just forget it."

"But I've just got to know about that archaeopteryx," he said. "It was absolutely amazing."

There was a long pause from up in her branch. Then, in a voice like a small child excited that her teacher had said he liked her drawing, she said, "It is pretty awesome, isn't it?"

"You've got to tell me how you got a proper DNA sample for it," Hank said. "You couldn't have simply taken it from a fossil. All the DNA there would have been degraded."

"Oh, you have no idea what I've discovered!" she said.

"Everyone always thinks that fossils don't preserve the DNA, and yet…" There was a long pause. "Wait, no. I'm not going to tell you that. Very tricky of you, though."

He supposed that was enough time for Morgan to get into place for whatever he was going to do, but Hank really wished he could somehow get Sanderton to start talking again. Whatever she had come up with must be infinitely more advanced than anything else that was out there. Maybe, just maybe, if she lived and was brought back to the states, she would give up her amazing secrets before she died.

Hank tried to see Morgan's current whereabouts, but the branches and leaves above them blocked his sight. After a few more seconds, though, he heard the clear sounds of a scuffle in the lower canopy. Just after that, the Kalashnikov dropped and bounced on the ground nearby them. Hank almost ran out to grab it, but he could see from here that the barrel had been damaged, and any attempt to fire it would likely end in the gun blowing up in his face.

"I think that's our cue," Hank whispered to Erin. The two of them burst from their cover, with Randy following as quickly as he could from his own hiding spot. Randy quickly fell behind, and both Hank and Erin had to go back and prop him up. It was evident that his wound was only getting worse, and all the running around was aggravating it to the point where Randy wouldn't be able to do much of anything soon. They had to get him to a spot where he could rest, or even pass out, but that didn't look like it was going to happen anytime soon.

There was a commotion behind them, and Hank looked back just in time to see two bodies falling through the leaves, vines and branches, bouncing between them all before they came to a stop on the ground. Morgan and Sanderton both groaned in pain at their fall, but there had been enough between them and the forest floor that neither of them looked like they had damaged anything vital.

Sanderton was the first to get up. She saw Morgan's machete where it had fallen next to them in the dirt and grabbed it, but she didn't immediately turn on the man that had ambushed her in the trees. Instead, she turned on Hank, Erin, and Randy.

"Mwahaha!" she screamed at them. It was probably intended as her version of an evil laugh, but it came out just sounding ridiculous.

"Quick, let's get off the path," Erin said, pulling Randy deeper into the thicker parts of the jungle. Hank, unsure of what she meant to accomplish, didn't dare let go of Randy, so he had no choice but to follow her. Erin chopped through the plants with her own machete, using her adrenaline to clear a path with almost inhuman speed. Behind them, however, Sanderton didn't have the same disadvantage. She could follow them easier through the path they had already made, and when Hank looked back, he could see that she was gaining on them quickly.

"Erin, if you have a plan here, you better get to it fast," Hank said.

"I think it's just up ahead," she said.

"You think?" Randy asked. "I would feel much better if you didn't qualify that statement."

"The river," Erin said. "If I'm remembering the maps right, this is the quickest way to the river."

Her memory did, in fact, serve them well. They came out of a particularly dense group of trees to find themselves at the water's edge.

"Okay, we're here," Hank said. "Now what?"

"Uhhh." Erin stared at the water ahead of them and apparently didn't like what she saw. "I don't see any sign of them. I was hoping they would be here."

"Hoping what would be here?" Hank asked.

Before Erin could respond, Sanderton came crashing out of

the rainforest behind them, her machete held high and ready to come down on their skulls. "Gotcha!" she said. "You didn't think I'd let you get away, right? My work is too important, too brilliant to let you..."

Hank saw the movement behind her just in time to yank Erin and Randy out of the way. Morgan launched himself out of the bushes and body-slammed Sanderton from behind. The machete slipped from her hand and whirled in the air until it landed in the mud tip-first, while both Sanderton and Morgan crashed into the river and rolled deeper into the water as they struggled.

"Look! There they are!" Erin said as she pointed to something farther out in the river. By this point, they all easily recognized the school of fish that was coming directly for the two people fighting each other in the water.

Morgan saw it, but rather than trying to get out the way, he wrapped an arm around Sanderton's neck and held her as steadily as he could in the water. Sanderton tried to scream, but it became a gurgle as she swallowed a mouthful of water. The captain held onto her firmly from behind as the shapes in the water got closer.

"Morgan, just let her go!" Hank screamed at him. "She's not worth your life!"

The water began to bubble in front of them with the approaching school of mutant piranhas. "You heard her," Morgan said. "If she gets away, she's just going to do it all over again."

Hank wanted to argue, but Morgan was right. Hank had heard her boast. Even if there was any chance that she wouldn't, the prions that had likely infected her brain wouldn't leave her alive for much longer anyway. She likely would live long enough, however, to go back to her research and try to create another *Titanoboa* again.

Against Hank's every instinct and better judgment, he gestured for Randy and Erin to follow him back in the direction of the path to the *Lucky Lucy*. However, no matter how hard he tried, he couldn't help looking back over his shoulder at what was happening in the water. Sanderton continued to fight, and as she did, Hank could see the honest fear in her eyes. Whatever the prions had done to her brain, in this moment, she was thinking clearly enough again to realize what was about to happen. The roiling water got closer, and the mutant piranhas got close enough to the surface that Hank could see their eyes and teeth. Sanderton screamed through a mouthful of water, and behind her Captain M. Morgan closed his eyes, preparing himself for what was about to come.

The first of the piranhas leaped out of the water, going right into Dr. Sanderton's face. Hank turned away, but not before he saw a splash of crimson, accompanied by Sanderton's gurgling scream. Morgan, however, didn't make a sound. If Hank hadn't already seen what these genetically modified piranhas had done to Stu, he might have even though Morgan could have gotten away. But the piranhas would be too fast, and Hank was sure that if he turned back to look again, he would see two gnawed-up skeletons sinking into the shallows.

His thoughts were so stuck on his friend's inevitable end that he didn't notice that his two remaining companions had stopped running until he slammed face-first into Randy's back. Hank almost said something rude in response, but Erin clapped a hand over his mouth.

"Don't speak," she whispered in his ear. "It might hear you."

Hank looked around her at the path between the camp and broken docks where they had moored the *Lucky Lucy*. He probably wouldn't have been able to see the boat from this distance under normal circumstances, but he most definitely could not now.

Right between them and their only method of escape, the *Titanoboa* had come to a rest. When curled up in a heap, it resembled little more than a mound of supple, scaled flesh. Its head was facing their direction, but both its eyes were closed. It was sleeping, but it completely blocked their escape. There was no way around it.

19

"Go back," Hank quietly whispered to the other two. "Back to the path we cut through the forest, then along the shoreline until we get to the boat."

Both Erin and Randy nodded silently. Slowly, carefully, the three of them started to back up. If the *Titanoboa* woke up while they were right in front of it, he had no doubt that at least one of them would die. He looked over at the other two and was reminded of how young they both were compared to him. Randy was a total ass, but he still had hopes and dreams, along with what should have been plenty of years yet to achieve them. Erin was far more dear to him, and Hank found that he truly didn't want to let her go, but if this came as a decision between which of them had to die, him or her, he suddenly knew exactly what he would do.

Hank looked back just long enough to make sure they weren't going to step on some stick that would snap and wake the monster up, but his precaution proved to be useless. When he looked back up at the snake in front of him, the creature's eyes were both open. Its tongue flicked out, tasting the air and picking up their scents.

"Oh crap," Erin said. The *Titanoboa* started to stir and

uncoil. It moved with deceptively slow speed at the moment, but Hank had already seen exactly how fast it could go when it wanted to. As soon as it was fully awake, the giant snake would inevitably strike, taking one of them for its dinner.

"Erin, go," Hank said. "Take Randy, and get as far away as you can."

"What?" Erin asked. "Oh no. I know what you're going to try doing. You're not sacrificing yourself for us."

"That's not my first inclination, if I can avoid it," Hank said. "Don't worry. I have a plan."

After a moment's hesitation, Erin nodded, then disappeared with Randy into the forest. He could hear her hacking away at the vines, but she was moving slower than she had just minutes earlier. Hank had to wonder if that was because she knew he was lying, that he didn't actually have a plan and had no hope that he was about to survive this.

The *Titanoboa* began to slither toward him. All it would take was one quick flick of its long, lithe body, and Hank would be crushed within the folds of its body. He wondered if he should close his eyes and just let it happen.

He thought again of Erin, of how much he cared for her, of how much time she still had left in her life and how much of that he could spend with her.

No. Screw just standing here and taking it. He was going to fight as long as he could breathe.

Hank recognized a twitch in the *Titanoboa*'s head that signaled it was about to strike. Right as it did, Hank sprang to the side, barely being missed by its mouth. Before he could think, before he could comprehend how crazy this was, Hank jumped at the snake and landed on its neck right behind the head.

The *Titanoboa* reared up, confused that its prey now seemed to be attacking it. Hank was just as perplexed, but he didn't dare let that get to him.

Don't let go, Hank thought to himself. *If you let go, I am definitely going to die, and the other two could die as well.* It wasn't like there was much of anything for him to hang on to, however. The *Titanoboa*'s scaly skin was smooth almost to the point of being greasy, and the head was wide enough that he had trouble gripping around the edges. The snake whipped its head to one side, almost managing to throw him off into the trees. Hank dug his knees into the side of its neck, allowing him to keep a hold on it for a few seconds more.

He heard a scream a short distance away, most likely from Randy as he fell yet again in his escape, and the noise also seemed to catch the interest of the *Titanoboa*.

"Oh no you don't," Hank said, then slammed his fist on the snake's eyebrow ridge. The *Titanoboa* jerked and shook its head again. This time, Hank lost his grip and slipped back down the snake's neck several feet before stopping himself. Oh, this was not good. This far down the snake's body, the *Titanoboa* would be able to twist its head around and pick him off like a dog chewing at a particularly meddlesome tick in its fur. The creature tried, but Hank twisted out of the way of its snapping jaws just in time. It hissed in what sounded suspiciously like frustration, then twisted its head away from him and started moving. Hank held on tight, but almost let go when he realized where the *Titanoboa* was going. It was heading right back through the path it had previously made through the forest, heading straight for the river. He had no idea of knowing exactly how smart the snake might be, but apparently it had just enough brains in its head to realize that the annoying thing clinging to it wouldn't be able to hold on in the water.

Not just into the water where it will be able to get me off and come at me, Hank thought, *but right where the piranhas could get me as well. I'm so screwed, unless…*

The piranhas. Holy hell, he knew exactly what he needed to

do. It would be dangerous and scary as shit, but it was the only way he believed he could take out the *Titanoboa*.

Leaves and branches whipped against Hank's face as the snake took him on a ride through the forest, with the natural foliage of the Amazon almost succeeding in getting him off where the creature had previously failed. Hank wished he had kept the machete instead of giving it to Erin, as he would probably be able to use it to stab the snake and, if not kill it, then at least use the blade as a handle to help him hold on.

There was a soft spot he could aim for though, he realized. Desperately pulling himself up the snake's neck again against the whipping branches in his face, Hank got up just behind the *Titanoboa*'s head. Ignoring how gross this was probably going to be, he rammed his hand directly into one of the snake's eyes. The hand encountered resistance for a moment before the eyeball popped and ejected vitreous fluid all down Hank's arm. The *Titanoboa* jerked again in an effort to be rid of him, then sped up right at the waterline. It skimmed through the shallower water, through the floodplain trees to a spot where the water was deep enough to start lapping at Hank's perch on the snake's back.

The fluid from the *Titanoboa*'s eye mixed with the murky water at the edge of the river. Hank hoped that would be enough. He looked over in the general direction of the river where he had last seen the school of piranhas killing Sanderton, hoping that they were already attracted to the sudden commotion in the water. Even if they weren't, Hank couldn't hang onto the *Titanoboa* any longer. His fingers slipped off from her hold, and he kicked away from the snake, hoping the momentum would be enough to push him a good distance back to the completely dry land.

It was, and he quickly found himself in the shallow muddy water that currently acted as the flooded river's shore. This would be too shallow for the piranhas to get him here, but he quickly realized he had a problem. The snake, realizing its nuisance was gone, had already turned around and looked like it was targeting Hank again. While this might have been a long distance to Hank, it wasn't so long that the *Titanoboa* wouldn't be able to cover that space nearly immediately, overtaking him and coiling around him in much the same way it had crushed poor Katherine.

"Hey, over here, you prehistoric phallic symbol son of a bitch!"

In a move that probably would have looked comical under any other circumstances, both Hank and the *Titanoboa* turned to look in the direction of the new voice at the exact same time. Hank actually started to choke in both triumph and revulsion at what he saw.

Captain M. Morgan, formerly of the *Lucky Lucy*, was standing in the shallows at the edge of the Amazon River, giving the *Titanoboa* the finger. And he looked like absolute shit.

He might have escaped from the piranhas that had ravaged Dr. Sanderton, but he most certainly hadn't gotten away unscathed. In fact, Hank had no idea how the man was still alive and walking on two legs. Huge chunks of flesh were missing from all over his body, and his clothes had been shredded to the point where he was almost naked. Blood flowed freely from every inch of him, and one of his eyes was missing. There was still enough of him left to smile, however, as he held up his machete and pointed it in the *Titanoboa*'s direction.

Before Hank could have any thoughts about trying to stop him, Morgan ran (or rather stumbled, given his current seriously wounded state) right through the shallows directly at the *Titanoboa*. He looked like a zombie, albeit a zombie still capable of decent speed and able to carry a weapon. He met the *Titanoboa* in a deeper section of the water just as the snake was about to lunge at him. Morgan swung the machete wildly and awkwardly, obviously affected by the extensive damage to his body, but the sharp side took a small chunk out of the

Titanoboa's snout, forcing it to pull back away from him. The *Titanoboa* still looked like it was going to try to eat the man once it figured out how to disarm him, but from the sight in the water beyond Morgan, Hank could see that he wouldn't need to hold off the snake for long. The super piranhas were coming, jumping and leaping over each other like they were competing to be the first one to reclaim their escaped prey.

Hank made his final scramble out of the water. A rustle of leaves to his right told him that Erin and Randy had found him again, meaning that all three of them were present to see the final, gruesome fight.

The free-for-all melee was incredibly difficult to make out, between the splashing water, spurting blood, incoherent screams both human and animal, and fast pace of it all. Hank was at least able to make out Morgan hacking away at the *Titanoboa*, scoring hit after hit in its thick hide and further polluting the water with blood to attract the piranhas. The snake hissed, twisted, and body slammed at its assailant, but none of it daunted Morgan. Even as the piranhas reached them both and attacked, he didn't let up. It wasn't until the *Titanoboa* dove for him headfirst with its jaws wide open that Morgan showed anything resembling fear, although that only lasted for a moment before his head went into the snake's maw. If there had been more time, Morgan would have joined Katherine digesting in the snake's belly, but with both of the combatants occupied, the piranhas were free to do their own thing. The *Titanoboa* appeared to realize only too late that its attention was on the wrong thing, and rather than trying to swallow the rabid demon of vengeance that had been going after it with a sword, it should have been running away from the smaller monsters attracted to its blood.

Instead, the *Titanoboa* was caught with a half-swallowed meal in its mouth as the blood-thirsty creatures found its every wound and cut, then exploited it to get at the soft, succulent flesh underneath. Most snakes, when confronted with an attack upon themselves in the middle of a feeding, would regurgitate their food and instead focus all their efforts on escape, but the *Titanoboa* didn't do that. Maybe that was part of the reason they had gone extinct, their inability to prioritize when their life was on the line, or maybe the *Titanoboa* was so used to being on the top of the food chain that it couldn't comprehend what was happening to it.

Morgan, his remains still dangling out of the *Titanoboa*'s mouth, shuddered with each attack from the piranhas, but Hank could have almost sworn he heard a disturbing noise coming from inside the *Titanoboa*'s throat.

It sounded like Captain Morgan was laughing.

Within a minute, there was nothing left identifiable of Morgan except bones and gristle hanging from the snake's mouth. A minute after that, the *Titanoboa* had been stripped of all its outer flesh.

The piranhas kept going, but at that point, Hank had to stop looking.

20

Hank, Erin, and Randy stood on the edge of the water, making sure to stay enough in the shallows that the super piranhas wouldn't be able to get at them without beaching themselves. The *Titanoboa* might have been gone, along with any hope of it ever breeding and creating more like it, but the piranhas were still loose, and likely always would be. They would breed soon, if they hadn't already, and would devastate the local ecology. For now, though, the creatures seemed to be sated as they lazily picked at the remaining pieces of meat from the *Titanoboa*'s skeleton.

There were two other skeletons in there as well, the captain's and the broken remains of what had once been Katherine, but Hank wouldn't let himself look at it.

"He sacrificed himself for us," Randy said with no little amount of wonder in his voice. "That ornery son of a bitch really did care."

"Of course he did," Hank said. It was a struggle to keep his voice from cracking. "That was just that way it was with Captain M. Morgan."

"You know, he never did tell us what the M stood for," Erin

said.

"He told me," Hank said. "It was Morgan."

Randy did a double-take. "I thought Morgan was his last name."

"It was," Hank said. "Morgan was both his first name and his last name."

"Jesus. Talk about sadistic parents," Erin said.

"Morgan Morgan. I almost wish I'd known so that I could have given him crap about it," Randy said.

"That's exactly why he didn't tell you," Hank said. "And why he didn't tell most people. Even I laughed. After that, he vowed never to tell anyone ever again, and he made me promise I would never reveal his first name until the day he died."

The significance of what he had just said hit him, and he had to choke back a sudden sob. He'd lost many people on this expedition, some he'd barely known, and others he had considered close personal friends. He wasn't entirely sure how to go on from here.

"We should get back to the *Lucky Lucy*," Erin said.

"Not that it's going to do any of us any good," Randy said. "Not only do none of us know how to pilot the damned thing, but it's more or less out of gas."

"We'll deal with each problem as we get to it," Hank said. "For now, with both Sanderton and the *Titanoboa* gone, what we really need to do is rest. Unless you want to try sleeping on the ground, the boat is the only place we're going to be able to do that."

Unfortunately for them, the *Lucky Lucy* was gone.

Hank had hoped that the cracking wood they'd heard so soon after getting on the island had either been a tree or the remains of the docks, but instead, they found that the *Titanoboa* had attacked the *Lucky Lucy*, thoroughly crushing it under its weight and coils and reducing most of the boat to little more than kindling. There might still be some parts that they would find salvageable among the wreckage, but most of that was now floating in the water, and none of them wanted to risk wading out when the piranhas could still be so close by.

"Well, I guess that's the end of us," Randy said. Interestingly, he sounded less upset than simply tired. Possibly, it was from the loss of blood, or maybe it was from the massive mental trauma they had all gone through. Or it could have been both. Whatever the cause, Randy plopped down at the edge of the water, his legs no longer able to hold him up.

Hank was about to say something in response – although he had no idea what might be helpful at this point in time – but stopped himself as he looked out at the river back the way they had originally come. At first, he almost thought that what he was seeing was a mirage, but as the seconds passed and the object got closer, he could no longer deny his eyes.

"It's a boat," he said softly to himself. Then, louder so that the other two could hear, "It's a boat!"

Whoever was in the boat must have seen them, since it changed course and started toward them. It appeared to be some kind of shipping boat. What it might be shipping, Hank didn't know and didn't care. All that mattered was that they did, in fact, have a way off this island.

Despite his bad leg, Randy stood up enough that he could wave his arms in an attempt to get the newcomer's attention. "Hey! Whoever you are, you've got to help us! Oh, uh, and don't shoot us, please."

As the boat got closer, someone responded in Brazilian-accented English. "Uh, why exactly would you think we would shoot you?"

Randy lowered his arms a little. "Uh, that's just the kind of days we've been having."

Hank could only imagine the sight they provided to the crew

of the approaching boat. Randy with his torn up and bleeding leg, him with barely any clothes thanks to them being ripped apart during his wild ride on the *Titanoboa*, and tiny little Erin with a machete in her hand, doing her best impersonation of a warrior princess. They probably looked like they had been surviving out in the wild for months rather than two days. Actually, come to think of it, they probably looked like a bunch of badasses.

"So, is this it?" Erin asked Hank as the boat pulled up near the shore. "Is this really the end of all your adventures in the Amazon?"

"You can't seriously be asking me that, right?" Hank asked. "I just watched friends and colleagues die in a variety of horrible ways. I can't come back here and do this again. Ever."

"And what if I said I wanted to do this from now on?" Erin asked.

"Even after everything that happened? You still think this might be your calling?"

"Yes, I do. But what I don't know is what that would mean for us. That is, if you even want there to be an us. I suppose this is the moment where you have to make your decision. Know that I'll accept if you want us to break it off, but I don't want that. I was telling you the truth when I said I love you."

So this was it, Hank realized. This was the moment where he had to make his decision. Not just about him and Erin, but about his life and where he would go from here. So what was more important to him: leaving behind the rigors of field work, work where people he knew and loved could quite possibly die, or being by the side of the young woman he loved?

Loved. That one word was enough to make the decision for him.

"And I love you too," Hank said. "I don't want to be without you. If that means doing more time in the field, then that's what will happen."

"Are you sure that's what you want?" Erin asked. "Even after everything that's happened?"

"I may be getting too old for the most rigorous aspects of fieldwork, but I'm sure there's got to be something I can still do as part of the support staff of a young, up-and-coming scientist. You wouldn't happen to know any, would you?"

Erin wrapped an arm around his waist. "I might know one."

Randy cleared his throat, and the two of them looked at him. "While I completely respect your need to get a room, might I suggest it wait until, oh, I don't know, we've all gotten proper medical attention, perhaps?"

Both Hank and Erin nodded. As the new arrivals searched for some place among the ruined docks to tie off, the three of them all sat down on the muddy shore, completely exhausted but fully aware of how lucky they were to still be alive.

THE END

CHECK OUT OTHER GREAT DINOSAUR THRILLERS

WRITTEN IN STONE
by **David Rhodes**

Charles Dawson is trapped 100 million years in the past. Trying to survive from day to day in a world of dinosaurs he devises a plan to change his fate. As he begins to write messages in the soft mud of a nearby stream, he can only hope they will be found by someone who can stop his time travel. Professor Ron Fontana and Professor Ray Taggit, scientists with opposing views, each discover the fossilized messages. While attempting to save Charles, Professor Fontana, his daughter Lauren and their friend Danny are forced to join Taggit and his group of mercenaries. Taggit does not intend to rescue Charles Dawson, but to force Dawson to travel back in time to gather samples for Taggit's fame and fortune. As the two groups jump through time they find they must work together to make it back alive as this fast-paced thriller climaxes at the very moment the age of dinosaurs is ending.

HARD TIME
by **Alex Laybourne**

Rookie officer Peter Malone and his heavily armed team are sent on a deadly mission to extract a dangerous criminal from a classified prison world. A Kruger Correctional facility where only the hardest, most vicious criminals are sent to fend for themselves, never to return.

But when the team come face to face with ancient beasts from a lost world, their mission is changed. The new objective: Survive.

SEVEREDPRESS

CHECK OUT OTHER GREAT DINOSAUR THRILLERS

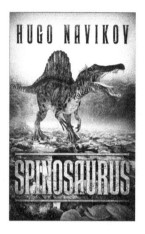

SPINOSAURUS
by Hugo Navikov

Brett Russell is a hunter of the rarest game. His targets are cryptids, animals denied by science. But they are well known by those living on the edges of civilization, where monsters attack and devour their animals and children and lay ruin to their shantytowns.

When a shadowy organization sends Brett to the Congo in search of the legendary dinosaur cryptid Kasai Rex, he will face much more than a terrifying monster from the past.

Spinosaurus is a dinosaur thriller packed with intrigue, action and giant prehistoric predators.

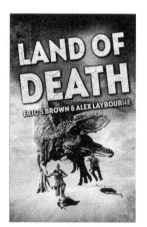

LAND OF DEATH
by Eric S Brown & Alex Laybourne

A group of American soldiers, fleeing an organized attack on their base camp in the Middle East, encounter a storm unlike anything they've seen before. When the storm subsides, they wake up to find themselves no longer in the desert and perhaps not even on Earth. The jungle they've been deposited in is a place ruled by prehistoric creatures long extinct. Each day is a struggle to survive as their ammo begins to run low and virtually everything they encounter, in this land they've been hurled into, is a deadly threat.

CHECK OUT OTHER GREAT DINOSAUR THRILLERS

JURASSIC ISLAND
by **Viktor Zarkov**

Guided by satellite photos and modern technology a ragtag group of survivalists and scientists travel to an uncharted island in the remote South Indian Ocean. Things go to hell in a hurry once the team reaches the island and the massive megalodon that attacked their boats is only the beginning of their desperate fight for survival.

Nothing could have prepared billionaire explorer Joseph Thornton and washed up archaeologist Christopher "Colt" McKinnon for the terrifying prehistoric creatures that wait for them on JURASSIC ISLAND!

K-REX
by **L.Z. Hunter**

Deep within the Congo jungle, Circuitz Mining employs mercenaries as security for its Coltan mining site. Armed with assault rifles and decades of experience, nothing should go wrong. However, the dangers within the jungle stretch beyond venomous snakes and poisonous spiders. There is more to fear than guerrillas and vicious animals. Undetected, something lurks under the expansive treetop canopy . . .

Something ancient.

Something dangerous.

Kasai Rex!

CPSIA information can be obtained
at www.ICGtesting.com
Printed in the USA
BVHW031919080720
583284BV00001B/167